Augustus J. C. (Augustus John Cuthbert) Hare

Biographical Sketches

Being Memorials of Arthur Penrhyn Stanley...Henry Alford...Mrs. Duncan Stewart,

etc

Augustus J. C. (Augustus John Cuthbert) Hare

Biographical Sketches
Being Memorials of Arthur Penrhyn Stanley...Henry Alford...Mrs. Duncan Stewart, etc

ISBN/EAN: 9783337019013

Printed in Europe, USA, Canada, Australia, Japan

Cover: Foto ©Raphael Reischuk / pixelio.de

More available books at **www.hansebooks.com**

BIOGRAPHICAL SKETCHES

BEING MEMORIALS OF

ARTHUR PENRHYN STANLEY, DEAN OF WESTMINSTER
HENRY ALFORD, DEAN OF CANTERBURY
MRS. DUNCAN STEWART

ETC.

BY

AUGUSTUS J. C. HARE

AUTHOR OF

"MEMORIALS OF A QUIET LIFE," "THE STORY OF TWO NOBLE LIVES,"
ETC.

LONDON
GEORGE ALLEN, 156, CHARING CROSS ROAD
1895

PREFACE

On the day after Arthur Stanley died, his only surviving sister and his most intimate friend, Hugh Pearson, wrote to me, asking me to be his biographer. I gladly accepted the office, as I felt sure that no one could know more of a cousin with whom much of my life had been spent, and to whose kindness—in my boyhood and youth—I had been most deeply indebted. But Sir George Grove, who was one of his literary executors, did not consider me competent for the work, and at first undertook to carry it out himself, afterwards intrusting it to others, whom—to the utmost of my power —I helped with materials. To myself, it was only left to write a magazine article, without any material but my own recollections and such letters as I personally possessed. It is given again here, in a slightly enlarged form, with illustrations. To this are added some memorials of my dear friend, Henry Alford, Dean of Canterbury, and of Mrs. Duncan Stewart, a clever and charming old lady, who was for some years a well-known figure in London society.[1]

AUGUSTUS J. C. HARE.

[1] The Article on Arthur Penrhyn Stanley first appeared in *Macmillan's Magazine*; that on Mrs. Duncan Stewart in *Good Words*; that on Paray le Monial in *Evening Hours*.

CONTENTS

LIST OF ILLUSTRATIONS

BIOGRAPHICAL SKETCHES

ARTHUR PENRHYN STANLEY

There are few country places in England which possess such a singular charm as Alderley. All who have lived in it have loved it, and to the Stanley family it has ever presented the ideal of that which is most interesting and beautiful. There the usually flat pasture-lands of Cheshire rise suddenly into the rocky ridge of Alderley Edge, with its Holy Well under an overhanging cliff, its gnarled pine-trees, and its storm-beaten beacon-tower ready to give notice of an invasion, looking far over the green plain to the smoke of Stockport and Macclesfield, which indicates the presence of great towns on the horizon. Beautiful are the beech-woods which clothe the western side of the Edge, and feather over mossy lawns to the mere, which receives a reflection of their gor-

A*

geous autumnal tints, softened by a blue haze on its still waters.

Beyond the mere and Lord Stanley's park, on the edge of the pasture-lands, are the church and its surroundings—a wonderfully harmonious group, encircled by trees, with the old timbered inn of the "Eagle and Child" at the corner of the lane which turns up to them.   In later times the church itself has undergone a certain amount of "restoration," but sixty years ago it was marvellously picturesque, its chancel mantled in ivy of massy folds, which, while they concealed the rather indifferent architecture, had a glory of their own very different from that of the clipped, ill-used ivy which we generally see on such buildings ; but the old clock-tower, the outside stone staircase leading to the Park pew, the crowded groups of large square, lichen-stained gravestones, the disused font in the churchyard overhung by a yew-tree, and the gable-ended schoolhouse at the gate, built of red sandstone, with grey copings and mullioned windows, were the same.

Close by was the rectory, with its garden— the "Dutch Garden," of many labyrinthine flower-beds—joining the churchyard. A low house, with a verandah, forming a wide balcony for the upper story, where bird-cages hung amongst the roses; its rooms and passages filled with pictures, books, and the old carved oak furniture, usually little sought after or valued in those days, but which the Rector delighted to pick up amongst his cottages.

This Rector, Edward Stanley, younger brother of the Sir John who was living at the Park, was a little man, active in figure and in movement, with dark, piercing eyes, rendered more remarkable by the snow-white hair which was characteristic of him even when very young. With the liveliest interest on all subjects— political, philosophical, scientific, theological; with inexhaustible plans for the good of the human race in general, but especially for the benefit of his parishioners and the amusement of his seven nieces at the Park, he was the most popular character in the country-side. To children he was indescribably delightful. There was nothing that he was not supposed to know—and indeed who was there who knew more than he of insect life, of the ways and habits of birds, of fossils and where to find them, of drawing, of etching on wood and lithographing on stone, of plants and gardens, of the construction of ships and boats, and of the thousand home manufactures of which he was a complete master?

In his thirty-first year Edward Stanley had married Catherine, eldest daughter of Oswald Leycester, afterwards Rector of Stoke-upon-Terne, of an old Cheshire family, which, through many generations, had been linked with that of the Stanleys in the intimacy of friendship and neighbourhood ; for Toft, the old seat of the Leycesters and the pleasantest of family homes, was only a few miles from Alderley.

At the time of her engagement, Catherine Leycester was only sixteen, and at the time of her marriage only eighteen, but from childhood she had been accustomed to form her own character by thinking, reading, and digesting what she read. Owing to her mother's ill-health, she had very early in life had the re-sponsibility of educating and training her sister, who was much younger than herself. She was the best of listeners, fixing her eyes upon the speaker, but saying little herself, so that her old uncle, Hugh Leycester, used to assert of her, " Kitty has much sterling gold, but gives no ready change." To the frivolity of an ordi-nary acquaintance, her mental superiority and absolute self-possession of manner must always have made her somewhat alarming ; but those who had the opportunity of penetrating be-neath the surface were no less astonished at

her originality and freshness of ideas, and her
keen, though quiet, enjoyment of life, its pursuits and friendships, than by the calm wisdom
of her advice, and her power of penetration

ALDERLEY RECTORY AND CHURCH.

into the characters, and consequently the temptations and difficulties, of others.

In the happy home of Alderley Rectory her
five children were brought up. Her eldest
son, Owen, had from the first shown that
interest in all things relating to ships and

naval affairs which had been his father's natural inclination in early life; and the youngest, Charles, from an early age had turned his hopes to the profession of a Royal Engineer, in which he afterwards became distinguished. Arthur, the second boy, born December 13, 1815, and named after the Duke of Wellington, was always delicate, so delicate that it was scarcely hoped at first he would live to grow up. From his earliest childhood, his passion for poetry, and historical studies of every kind, gave promise of a literary career, and engaged his mother's unwearied interest in the formation of his mind and character. A pleasant glimpse of the home life at Alderley in May, 1818, is given in a letter from Mrs. Stanley to her sister, Maria Leycester :—

"How I have enjoyed these fine days,—and one's pleasure is doubled, or rather I should say trebled, in the enjoyment of the three little children basking in the sunshine on the lawns and picking up daisies and finding new flowers every day,—and in seeing Arthur expand like one of the flowers in the fine weather. Owen trots away to school at nine o'clock every morning, with his Latin grammar under his arm, leaving Mary with a strict charge to unfurl his flag, which he leaves carefully furled, through the little gothic gate, as soon as the clock strikes twelve. So Mary unfurls the flag and then watches till Owen comes in sight, and as soon as he spies her signal he sets off full gallop towards it, and Mary creeps through the gate to meet him, and then comes with as much joy to announce Owen's being come back, as if he was returned from the North Pole. Meanwhile I am sitting with the doors open into the trellis, so that I can see and hear all that passes."

In the same year, after an absence, Mrs. Stanley wrote :—

"*Alderley, Sept.* 14, 1818.—What happy work it was getting home! The little things were as happy to see us as we could desire. They all came dancing out, and clung round me, and kissed me by turns, and were certainly more delighted than they had ever been before to see us again. They had not only not forgot us, but not forgot a bit about us. Everything that we had done and said and written was quite fresh and present to their minds, and I should be assured in vain that all my trouble in writing to them was thrown away. Arthur is grown so interesting, and so entertaining too,—he talks incessantly, runs about and amuses himself, and is full of pretty speeches, repartees, and intelligence : the dear little creature would not leave me, or stir without holding my hand, and he knew all that had been going on quite as much as the others. He is more like Owen than ever, only softer, more affectionate, and not what you call ' so fine a boy.' "

When he was four years old, we find his mother writing to her sister :—

"*January* 30, 1820.—As for the children, my Arthur is sweeter than ever. His drawing fever goes on, and his passion for pictures and birds, and he will talk sentiment to Mademoiselle about *le printemps, les oiseaux,* and *les fleurs,* when he walks out. When he went to Highlake, he asked—quite gravely—whether it would not be good for his little wooden horse to have some sea-bathing!"

And again, in the following summer :—

"*Alderley, July* 6, 1820.—I have been taking a domestic walk with the three children and the pony to Owen's favourite cavern, Mary and Arthur taking it in turns to ride. Arthur was sorely puzzled between his fear and his curiosity. Owen and Mary, full of adventurous spirit, went with Mademoiselle to explore. Arthur stayed with me and the pony, but when I said I would go, he said, colouring, he would go, he thought : 'But, Mamma, do you think there are any wild dogs in the cavern ? ' Then we picked up various specimens of cobalt, &c., and we carried them in a basket, and we called at Mrs. Barber's, and we got some string, and we tied the basket to the pony with some trouble, and we got home very safe, and I finished the delights of the evening by reading 'Paul and Virginia' to Owen and Mary, with which they were much delighted, and so was I.

"You would have given a good deal for a peep at Arthur this evening, making hay with all his little strength—such a beautiful colour, and such soft animation in his blue eyes."

It was often remarked that Mrs. Stanley's children were different from those of any one else; but this was not to be wondered at. Their mother not only taught them their lessons, she learnt all their lessons with them. Whilst other children were plodding through dull histories of disconnected countries and ages, of which they were unutterably weary at the time, and of which they remembered nothing afterwards, Mrs. Stanley's system was to take a particular era, and, upon the basis of its general history, to pick out for her children from different books, whether memoirs, chronicles, or poetry, all that bore upon it, making it at once an interesting study to herself and them, and talking it over with them in a way which encouraged them to form their own opinion upon it, to have theories as to how such-and-such evils might have been forestalled or amended, and so to fix it in their recollection.

To an imaginative child, Alderley was the most delightful place possible, and whilst Owen Stanley delighted in the clear brook which dashes through the Rectory garden for the ships of his own manufacture—then as engrossing as the fitting out of the *Ariel* upon the mere in later boyhood—little Arthur

revelled in the legends of the neighbourhood—
of its wizard of Alderley Edge, with a hundred
horses sleeping in an enchanted cavern, and of
the church-bell which fell down a steep hill
into Rostherne Mere, and which is tolled by
a mermaid when any member of a great neighbouring family is going to die.

Being the poet of the little family, Arthur
Stanley generally put his ideas into verse, and
there are lines of his written at eleven years old,
on seeing the sunrise from the top of Alderley church-tower, and at twelve years old, on
witnessing the departure of the *Ganges*, bearing his brother Owen from Spithead, which
give evidence of poetical power, more fully
evinced two years later in his longer poems
on "The Druids" and on "The Maniac of
Betharam." When he was old enough to go
to school, his mother wrote an amusing account
of the turn-out of his pockets and desk before
leaving home, and the extraordinary collection
of crumpled scraps of poetry which were found
there. In March 1821 Mrs. Stanley wrote :—

"Arthur is in great spirits, and looks well prepared
to do honour to the jacket and trousers preparing for
him. He is just now opposite to me, lying on the
sofa (his lesson being concluded) reading Miss Edge-
worth's 'Frank' to himself most eagerly. I must

tell you his moral deductions from 'Frank.' The other day, as I was dressing, Arthur, Charlie, and Elizabeth were playing in the passage. I heard a great crash, which turned out to be Arthur running very fast, not stopping himself in time, and coming against the window at the end of the passage, so as to break three panes. He was not hurt, but I heard Elizabeth remonstrating with him on the crime of breaking windows, to which he answered with great *sang-froid*, 'Yes, but you know Frank's mother said she would rather have all the windows in the house broke than that Frank should tell a lie: so now I can go and tell Mamma, and then I shall be like Frank.' I did not make my appearance, so when the door opened for the *entrée* after dinner, Arthur came in first in something of a bustle, with cheeks as red as fire, and eyes looking—as his eyes do look—saying the instant the door opened, 'Mamma! I have broke three panes of glass in the passage window:—and I tell you now 'cause I was afraid to forget.' I am not sure whether there is not a very inadequate idea left on his mind as to the sin of glass-breaking, and that he rather thought it a fine thing having the opportunity of coming to tell Mamma something like Frank; however, there was some little effort, *vide* the agitation and red cheeks, so we must not be hypercritical."

After he was eight years old, Mrs. Stanley, who knew the interest and capacity of her little Arthur about everything, was much troubled by his becoming so increasingly shy, that he

never would speak if he could help it, even
when he was alone with her, and she dreaded
that the companionship of other boys at school,
instead of drawing him out, would only make
him shut himself up more within himself. Still,
in the frequent visits which his parents paid to
the seaside at Highlake, he always recovered
his lost liveliness of manner and movement,
climbed merrily up the sandhills, and was never
tired in mind or body. It was therefore a
special source of rejoicing when it was found
that Mr. Rawson the Vicar of Seaforth (a place
five miles from Liverpool, and only half a mile
from the sea), had a school for nine little boys,
and thither in 1824 it was decided that Arthur
should be sent. In August his young aunt
wrote :—

" Arthur liked the idea of going to school, as making
him approach nearer to Owen. We took him last
Sunday evening from Crosby, and he kept up very
well till we were to part, but when he was to separate
from us to join his new companions, he clung to us in
a piteous manner and burst into tears. Mr. Rawson
very good-naturedly offered to walk with us a little
way, and walk back with Arthur, which he liked
better, and he returned with Mr. R. very manfully.
On Monday evening we went to have a look at him
before leaving the neighbourhood, and found the little
fellow as happy as possible, much amused with the

novelty of the situation, and talking of the boys' proceedings with as much importance as if he had been
there for months. He wished us good-bye in a very
firm tone, and we have heard since from his Uncle
Penrhyn that he had been spending some hours with
him, in which he laughed and talked incessantly of
all that he did at school. He is very proud of being
called 'Stanley,' and seems to like it altogether very
much. The satisfaction to Mamma and Auntie is not
to be told of having disposed of this little sylph in so
excellent a manner. Every medical man has always
said that a few years of constant sea-air would make
him quite strong, and to find this united to so desirable a master as Mr. R., and so careful and kind a
protectress as Mrs. R., is being very fortunate."

In the following summer the same pen writes
from Alderley to one of the family :—

"*July* 1825.—You know how dearly I love all these
children, and it has been such a pleasure to see them
all so happy together—Owen, the hero upon whom all
their little eyes were fixed, and the delicate Arthur
able to take his own share of boyish amusements with
them, and telling out his little store of literary wonders
to Charlie and Catherine. School has not transformed
him into a rough boy yet. He is a little less shy, but
not much. He brought back from school a beautiful
prize-book for history, of which he is not a little proud;
and Mr. Rawson has told several people, unconnected
with the Stanleys, that he never had a more amiable,
attentive, or clever boy than Arthur Stanley, and that

he never has had to find fault with him since he came.
My sister finds, in examining him, that he not only
knows what he has learnt himself, but that he picks
up all the knowledge gained by the other boys in their
lessons, and can tell what each boy in the school has
read, &c. His delight in reading 'Madoc' and 'Thalaba'
is excessive."

In the following year Miss Leycester
writes :—

"*Stoke, August* 26, 1826.—My Alderley children
are more interesting than ever.   Arthur is giving Mary
quite a literary taste, and is of the greatest advantage
to her possible, for they are now quite inseparable
companions, reading, drawing, and writing together.
Arthur has written a poem on the life of a peacock-
butterfly in the Spenserian stanza, with all the old
words, with references to Chaucer, &c., at the bottom
of the page ! To be sure, it would be singular if they
were not different from other children, with the advan-
tages they have where education is made so interesting
and amusing as it is to them. . . . I never saw anything equal to Arthur's memory and quickness in
picking up knowledge ; seeming to have just the sort
of intuitive sense of everything relating to books that
Owen had in ships,—and then there is such affection
and sweetness of disposition in him. . . . You will not
be tired of all this detail of those so near my heart.   It
is always such a pleasure to me to write of the Rectory,
and I can always do it better when I am away from it
and it rises before my mental vision."

The summer of 1826 was marked for the Stanleys by the news of the death of their beloved friend Reginald Heber, and by the marriage of Isabella Stanley to Captain Parry, the Arctic voyager, an event at which his

ALDERLEY MERE.

mother "could not resist sending for her little Arthur to be present." Meantime he was happy at school, and wrote long histories home of all that took place there, especially amused with his drilling sergeant, who told him to "put

on a bold, swaggering air, and not to look
sheepish." But each time of his return to
Alderley he seemed shier than ever, and his
mother became increasingly concerned at his
want of boyishness. His cousin Emma Tatton,
afterwards Lady Mainwaring, recollected how,
when a large party of children were playing
together, she said, "Now, Arthur, you must
come and play at trap and ball."—"But I can't,
Cousin Emma," the boy answered, hanging
down his hands and head. "But you must."
—"No, Cousin Emma, I really can't."—"Well
then, Arthur, I'll tell you what, I'll let you off,
if you'll go at once and write me an ode to a
Snowdrop and give it to me to-morrow morning at breakfast;" and the next morning it was
ready. Here is a paraphase of Psalm cxxxix.
which he wrote at twelve years old (1827):—

> "If up to heav'n I wing my flight,
> And seek the realms of endless light,
> There Thy eternal glories shine,
> And all is holy, all divine,
> All free from sin, and pain, and care,
> For, full of mercy, Thou art there !
>
> If I descend to deepest hell,
> Where evil souls for ever dwell
> And bitterly lament their woe,
> While torturing fires for ever glow,
> Thy dreadful vengeance there I fear,
> For Thou, O mighty Lord, art there !

If through the ocean's path I stray,
And o'er its surface urge my way,
If blows the wind, if mounts the wave,
Thy strong right hand can always save,
Though many storms obscure the air,
For, wrapt in tempests, Thou art there !

If, wand'ring from my native home,
To earth's remotest verge I come,
Where everlasting winter reigns
And binds the seas in icy chains,
Or where the sun-scorched deserts glare,
In heat or cold, Thou, Lord, art there !

Whether the rosy morning rise
With radiance on the gladdened skies,
Or noon shed forth his burning ray,
Or evening bring the close of day,
Thy glories through the world appear,
For Thou, O gracious Lord, art there !

In vain amid the darkest night
I would escape Thy piercing sight :
Thou through the deepest shade can'st see,
And darkness is as light to Thee,
E'en as the brightest noontide glare,
For Thou, omniscient God, art there !

Where from Thy presence shall I fly ?
Where hide from Thy all-searching eye ?
My deeds are still before Thy face,
Thy goodness is in every place :
Thy bounteous grace is ever near,
For Thou, O Lord, art everywhere !"

B

We find Mrs. Stanley writing:—

"*January* 27, 1828.—Oh, it is so difficult to know how to manage Arthur. He takes having to learn dancing so terribly to heart, and enacts Prince Pitiful; and will, I am afraid, do no good at it. Then he thinks I do not like his reading because I try to draw him *also* to other things, and so he reads by stealth, and lays down his book when he hears people coming; and having no other pursuits or anything he cares for but reading, has a listless look, and I am sure he is very often unhappy. I suspect, however, that this is Arthur's worst time, and that he will be a happier man than boy."

In January 1828 Mrs. Stanley wrote to Augustus W. Hare, long an intimate friend of the family, and soon about to marry her sister :—

" I have Arthur at home, and I have rather a puzzling card to play with him—how not to encourage too much his poetical tastes, and to spoil him, in short—and yet how not to discourage what in reality one wishes to grow, and what he, being timid and shy to a degree, would easily be led to shut up entirely to himself; and then he suffers so much from a laudable desire to be with other boys, and yet, when with them, finds his incapacity to enter into their pleasures of shooting, hunting, horses, and take theirs for his. He will be happier as a man, as literary men are more within reach than literary boys."

In the following month she wrote :—

"*Alderley, February* 8, 1828.—Now I am going to ask your opinion and advice, and perhaps your assistance, on my own account. We are beginning to consider what is to be done with Arthur, and it will be time for him to be moved from his small school in another year, when he will be thirteen. We have given up all thoughts of Eton for him from the many objections, combined with the great expense. Now I want to ask your opinion about Shrewsbury, Rugby, and Winchester; do you think, from what you know of Arthur's character and capabilities, that Winchester would suit him, and *vice versâ?*"

In answer to this Augustus Hare wrote to her from Naples :—

"*March* 26, 1828.—Are you aware that the person of all others fitted to get on with boys is just elected master of Rugby? His name is Arnold. He is a Wykehamist and Fellow of Oriel, and a particular friend of mine—a man calculated beyond all others to engraft modern scholarship and modern improvements on the old-fashioned stem of a public education. Winchester under him would be the best school in Europe; what Rugby may turn out I cannot say, for I know not the materials he has there to work on."

A few weeks later he added :—

"*Florence, April* 19, 1828.—I am so little satisfied with what I said about Arthur in my last letter, that I am determined to begin with him and do him more justice. What you describe him now to be, I once was; and I have myself suffered too much and too often from my inferiority in strength and activity to boys who were superior to me in nothing else, not to feel very deeply for any one in a similar state of school-forwardness and bodily weakness. Parents in general are too anxious to push their children on in school and other learning. If a boy happens not to be robust, it is laying up for him a great deal of pain and mortification. For a boy must naturally associate with others in the same class; and consequently, if he happens to be forward beyond his years, he is thrown at twelve (with perhaps the strength of only eleven or ten) into the company of boys two years older, and probably three or four years stronger (for boobies are always stout of limb). You may conceive what wretchedness this is likely to lead to, in a state of society like a school, where might almost necessarily makes right. But it is not only at school that such things lead to mortification. There are a certain number of manly exercises which every gentleman, at some time or other of his life, is likely to be called on to perform, and many a man who is deficient in these would gladly purchase dexterity in them, if he could, at the price of those mental accomplishments which have cost him in boyhood the most pains to acquire. Who would not rather ride well at twenty-five than write the prettiest Latin verses? I am perfectly impartial in this respect, being able to do neither, and therefore my judgment is likely enough to be correct. So pray during the holidays make Arthur ride hard and shoot often, and, in short, gymnasticise in every possible manner. I have said thus much to relieve my own mind, and convey to you how earnestly I feel on the subject. Otherwise I know Alderley and its inhabitants too well to suspect any one of them of being what Wordsworth calls 'an intellectual all-in-all.' About his school, were Rugby under any other master, I certainly should not advise your thinking of it for Arthur for an instant; as it is, the decision will be more difficult. When Arnold has been there ten years, he will have made it a good school, perhaps in some respects the very best in the island; but a transition state is always one of doubt and delicacy. Winchester is admirable for those it succeeds with, but it is not adapted for all sorts and conditions of boys, and sometimes fails. However, when I come to England, I will make a point of seeing Arthur, when I shall be a little better able perhaps to judge."

In the summer of 1828 Mr. and Mrs. Stanley, with her sister Maria and her niece Lucy Stanley from the Park, went by sea to Bordeaux and for a tour in the Pyrenees, taking little Arthur and his sister Mary with them. It was his first experience of foreign travel, and most intense was his enjoyment of it. All was new then, and Mr. Stanley wrote of the children as being almost as much intoxicated with delight on first landing at Bordeaux as their faithful maid, Sarah Burgess, who "thinks life's fitful dream is past, and that she has, by course of transmigration, passed into a higher sphere." It is recollected how, when he first saw the majestic summit of the Pic du Midi rising above a mass of cloud, Arthur Stanley in his great ecstasy flung himself on the ground exclaiming, "What shall I do! what shall I do!" He described his impressions afterwards in a poem on the Maladetta—one of the many poems he wrote as a child. His father's knowledge of geology had given it such a weird interest that nothing in after-life impressed him more. "It was so awful," he wrote in his journal, "thinking that this mighty Maladetta had burst up out of the earth, driving every other mountain before it; and, as one looked round, seeing them all leaning away from it, as if they shrank in terror from their king."

In the following October Mrs. Stanley described her boy's peculiarities to Dr. Arnold, and asked his candid advice as to how far Rugby was likely to suit him. After receiving his answer she wrote to her sister :—

"*October* 10, 1828.—Dr. Arnold's letter has decided us about Arthur. I should think there was not another schoolmaster in his Majesty's dominions who would write such a letter. It is so lively, agreeable, and promising in all ways. He is just the man to take a fancy to Arthur, and for Arthur to take a fancy to."

It was exactly as his mother had foreseen. Arthur Stanley went to Rugby in the following January, a bright and eager, but timid and delicate little boy, in a "many-buttoned" blue jacket, frills, and a pink watch-ribbon. He was immediately captivated by his new master. "I should never have taken him for a doctor; he was very pleasant, and does not look old," he wrote to his sister Mary after his first sight of Arnold, who was the man of all others suited to stimulate the best type of English boy. Soon Arthur wrote home that, though he had a great sense of desolation at school, he had "no miseries." Indeed, like many other nervous boys, he was astonished to find that school existence was not very unlike life everywhere else, for, as he wrote afterwards to a school companion, he had looked forward to a long farewell to all goodness and happiness, and wondered how he should ever come out safe."

Two months after Arthur Stanley's entrance at Rugby, his parents visited him as they were returning from Cheshire to London. Mrs. Stanley wrote to her sister :—

"*March* 1829.—We arrived at Rugby exactly at twelve, waited to see the boys pass, and soon spied Arthur with his books on his shoulder. He coloured up and came in, looking very well, but cried a good deal on seeing us, chiefly I think from nervousness. The only complaint he had to make was that of having no friend, and the feeling of loneliness belonging to that want, and this, considering what he is and what boys of his age usually are, would and must be the case everywhere. We went to dine with Dr. and Mrs. Arnold, and they are of the same opinion, that he was as well off and as happy as he could be at a public school, and on the whole I am satisfied—quite satisfied considering all things, for Dr. and Mrs. Arnold are indeed delightful. She was ill, but still animated and lively. He has a very remarkable countenance, something in forehead, and again in manner, which puts me in mind of Reginald Heber, and there is a mixture of zeal, energy, and determination tempered with wisdom, candour, and benevolence, both in manner and in everything he says. He has examined Arthur's class, and said Arthur has done very well, and the class generally. He said he was gradually reforming, but that it was like pasting down a piece of paper—as fast as one corner was put down another started up. 'Yes,' said Mrs. A., 'but Dr. Arnold always thinks the corner will not start *again*.' And it is that happy sanguine temperament which is so particularly calculated to do well in this, or indeed any situation."

Soon Arthur Stanley became very happy at Rugby. From the first he had given evidence

of his distinctive individuality. He was in his
element when he was elected first President of
a Debating Society, but it was in vain that once
or twice he tried to think he liked playing at
football. "Perhaps in time I may like cricket,"
he wrote to Alderley, where he thought it would
give pleasure ; but he never did, he always hated
it. He hated mathematics and arithmetic too ;
only one boy, indeed, was ever remembered
more utterly hopeless about arithmetic than
Arthur Stanley : it was W. E. Gladstone, afterwards Chancellor of the Exchequer ! Stanley's
physical peculiarities alone made him different
from other boys. Through life, the senses of
smell and taste were utterly unknown to him ;
once only—in Switzerland—he fancied he smelt
the freshness of a pine-wood. "It made the
world a paradise," he said.

But though he never understood school ways,
Arthur Stanley's school-fellows respected the
peculiarities of "the child of light," as Matthew
Arnold called him, and left him alone—like a dog
of another nature. His study became known
as the "Poet's Corner," and from it he was able
to announce prize after prize to the home circle,
to whom his letters were rapidly becoming one
of the most interesting things of life. Want
of a friend was speedily supplied at Rugby,

and many of the friends of his whole after-life
dated from his early school days, especially
Charles Vaughan, afterwards his intimate companion, eventually his brother-in-law. His
rapid removal into the shell at Easter, and into
the fifth form at Midsummer, brought him
nearer to the head-master, at the same time
freeing him from the terrors of preposters and
fagging, and giving him entrance to the library.
So he returned to Alderley in the summer
holidays well and prosperous, speaking out and
full of fun and happiness, ready to enjoy
" striding about upon the lawn on stilts " with
his brother and sisters. On his return to school,
his mother continued to hear of his progress in
learning, but derived even more pleasure from
his accounts of football, and of a hare-and-
hounds hunt in which he "got left behind with
a clumsy boy and a silly one " at a brook, which,
after some deliberation, he leapt, and *nothing
happened*."

In September 1829 his mother writes :—

" I have had such a ridiculous account from Arthur
of his sitting up, with three others, all night, *to see
what it was like!* They heartily wished themselves
in bed before morning. He also writes of an English
copy of verses given to the fifth form—Brownsover, a
village near Rugby, with the Avon flowing through

it and the Swift flowing into the Avon, into which
Wickliffe's ashes were thrown. So Arthur and some
others instantly made a pilgrimage to Brownsover to
make discoveries. They were allowed four days, and
Arthur's was the best of the thirty in the fifth form,
greatly to his astonishment, but, he says, 'Nothing
happened, except that I get called Poet now and then,
and my study, Poet's Corner.' The master of the
form gave another subject for them to write upon in
an hour, to see if they had each made their own, and
Arthur was again head. What good sense there is
in giving subjects of that kind to excite interest and
inquiry, though few would be so supremely happy as
Arthur in making the voyage of discovery. I ought
to mention that Arthur was detected with the other
boys in an unlawful letting off of squibs, and had a
hundred lines of Horace to translate!"

The following gleanings from his mother's
letters give, in the absence of other material,
glimpses of Arthur Stanley's life during the
next few years :—

"*February* 22, 1830.—Arthur writes me word he has
begun mathematics, and does not wonder Archimedes
never heard the soldiers come in if he was as much
puzzled over a problem as he is."

"*June* 1, 1830.—We got to Rugby at eight, fetched
Arthur, to his great delight and surprise, and had two
most comfortable hours with him. There is just a
shade more of confidence in his manners, which is very
becoming. He talked freely and fluently, looked well

and happy, and came the next morning at six o'clock with his Greek book and his notebook under his arm."

"*June* 22, 1830.—There was a letter from Arthur on Monday, saying that his verses on Malta had failed in getting the prize. There had been a hard contest between him and another. His poem was the longest and contained the best ideas, but he says 'that is matter of opinion;' the other was the most accurate. There were three masters on each side, and it was some time in being decided. The letter expresses his disappointment (for he had thought he should have it), his vexation (knowing that another hour would have enabled him to look over, and probably to correct the fatal faults), so naturally, and then the struggle of his amiable feeling that it would be unkind to the other boy, who had been very much disappointed not to get the Essay, to make any excuses. Altogether it is just as I should wish, and much better than if he had got it."

"*July* 20, 1830.—Arthur came yesterday. He begins to look like a young man."

"*December* 1830.—Arthur has brought home a letter from Mrs. Arnold to say that she could not resist sending me her congratulations on his having received the remarkable distinction of not being examined at all except in extra subjects. Dr. Arnold called him up before masters and school, and said he had done so perfectly well it was useless."

"*December* 30, 1830.—I was so amused the other day taking up the memorandum-books of my two boys. Owen's full of calculations, altitudes, astronomical axioms, &c. Arthur's of Greek idioms, Grecian history, parallels of different historical situations. Owen does Arthur a great deal of good by being so much more attentive and civil; it piques him to be more alert. Charlie profits by both brothers. Arthur examines him in his Latin, and Charlie sits with his arm round his neck, looking with the most profound deference in his face for exposition of Virgil."

"*February* 1831.—Charlie writes word from school: 'I am very miserable, not that I want anything, except to be at home.' Arthur does not mind going half so much. He says he does not know why, but all the boys seem fond of him, and he never gets plagued in any way like the others; his study is left untouched, his things unbroke, his books undisturbed. Charlie is so fond of him, and deservedly so. You would have been so pleased one night, when Charlie all of a sudden burst into violent distress at not having finished his French task for the holidays, by Arthur's judicious good-nature in showing him how to help himself, entirely leaving what he was about of his own employment."

"*July* 1831.—I am writing in the midst of an academy of art. Just now there are Arthur and Mary drawing and painting at one table; Charlie deep in the study of fishes and hooks, and drawing varieties of both at another; and Catherine with her slate full of houses with thousands of windows. Charlie is fishing mad, and knows how to catch every sort, and just now he informs me that to catch a bream you must go out before breakfast. He is just as fond as ever of Arthur. You would like to see Arthur examine him, which he does so mildly and yet so strictly, explaining everything so à *l'Arnold*."

"*July* 17, 1831.—I have been busy teaching Arthur to drive, row, and gymnasticise, and he finds himself making progress in the latter; that he can do more as he goes on—a great encouragement always. Imagine Dr. Arnold and one of the other masters gymnasticising in the garden, and sometimes going out leaping—as much a sign of the times as the Chancellor appearing without a wig, and the king with half a coronation."

"*Alderley, November* 11.—We slept at Rugby on Monday night, had a comfortable evening with Arthur, and next morning breakfasted with Dr. Arnold. What a man he is! He struck me more than before even with the impression of power—energy, and single-ness of heart, aim, and purpose. He was very indig-nant at the *Quarterly Review* article on cholera—the surpassing selfishness of it, and spoke so *nobly*—was busy writing a paper to state what cholera is, and what it is not. . . . Arthur's veneration for him is beautiful; what good it must do to grow up under such a tree."

"*December* 22, 1831.—I brought Arthur home on Wednesday from Knutsford. He was classed first in everything but composition, in which he was second, and mathematics, in which he did not do well enough to be classed, nor ill enough to prevent his having the reward of the rest of his works. I can trace the improvement from his having been so much under Dr. Arnold's influence; so many inquiries and ideas are started in his mind which will be the groundwork of future study. . . . Charlie is very happy now in the thought of going to Rugby and being with Arthur, and Arthur has settled all the study and room concerns very well for him. I am going to have a sergeant from Macclesfield to drill them these holidays, to Charlie's great delight, and Arthur's patient endurance. The latter wants it much. It is very hard always to be obliged to urge that which is against the grain. I never feel I am doing my duty so well to Arthur as when I am teaching him to dance, and urging him to gymnasticise, when I would so much rather be talking to him of his notebooks, &c. He increasingly needs the free use of his powers of mind too as well as of his body. The embarrassments and difficulty of getting *out* what he knows seems so painful to him, while some people's pain is all in getting it in; but it is very useful for him to have drawbacks in everything."

"*May* 22, 1832.—We got such a treat on Friday evening in Arthur's parcel of prizes. One copy he had illustrated in answer to my questions, with all his authorities, to show how he came by the various bits of information. In this parcel he sent ' An Ancient Ballad, showing how Harold the King died at Chester,' the result of a diligent collation of old chronicles he and Mary had made together in the winter. Arthur put all the facts together from memory."

"*Dec.* 26, 1832.—Arthur and Charlie came home on Wednesday. Arthur has not shaken off his first fit of shyness yet. I think he colours more than ever, and hesitates more in bringing out what he has to say. I am at my usual work of teaching him to use his body, and Charlie his mind."

"*April* 13, 1833.—I never found Arthur more blooming than when we saw him at Rugby on Monday. Mrs. Arnold said she always felt that Arthur had more sympathy with her than any one else, that he understood and appreciated Dr. Arnold's character, and the union of strength and tenderness in it; that Dr. A. said he always felt that Arthur took in his ideas, received all he wished to put into him more in the true spirit and meaning than any boy he had ever met with, and that she always delighted in watching his countenance when Dr. Arnold was preaching."

"*July* 1833.—At eight o'clock last night the Arnolds arrived. Dr. Arnold and Arthur behind the carriage, Mrs. Arnold and two children inside, two more with the servant in front, having left the other chaiseful at Congleton. Arthur was delighted with his journey—said Dr. Arnold was just like a boy—jumped up, delighted to be set free—had talked all the way of the geology of the country, knowing every step of it by heart—so pleased to see a common, thinking it might do for the people to expatiate on. We talked of the Cambridge philosophers—why he did not go there—he dared not trust himself with its excitement or with society in London. Edward said something of the humility of finding yourself with people so much your superior, and at the same time the elevation of feeling yourself of the same species. He shook his head —' I should feel that in the company of legislators, but not of abstract philosophers.' Then Mrs. Arnold went on to say how Deville had pronounced on his head that he was fond of *facts*, but not of abstractions, and he allowed it was most true ; he liked geology, botany, philosophy only as they are connected with the history and well-being of the human race. . . . The other chaise came after breakfast. He ordered all into their places with such a gentle decision, and they were all off by ten, having ascertained, I hope, that it was quite worth while to halt here even for so short a time."

It was in November 1833 that Arthur Stanley went to Oxford to try for the Balliol Scholarship, and gained the first scholarship against thirty competitors. The examination was one especially calculated to show the wide range of Arnold's education. Stanley wrote from Oxford to his family :—

" *November* 26, 1833.—On Monday our examination began at 10 A.M. and lasted to 4 P.M.—a Latin theme, which, as far as four or five revisals could make sure, was without mistakes, and satisfied me pretty well. In the evening we went in from 7 P.M. till 10, and had a Greek chorus to be translated with notes, and also turned into Latin verses, which I did not do well. On Tuesday from 10 to 1 we had an English theme and a criticism on Virgil, which I did pretty well, and Greek verses from 2 to 4—middling, and we are to go in again to-night at 9. I cannot the least say if am likely to get it. There seem to be three formidable competitors, especially one from Eton."

" *Friday, November* 29, 7¼ P.M.—I will begin my letter in the midst of my agony of expectation and fear. I finished my examination to-day at two o'clock. At 8 to-night the decision takes place, so that my next three-quarters of an hour will be dreadful. As I do not know how the other schools have done, my hope of success can depend upon nothing, except that I think I have done pretty well, better perhaps from comparing notes than the rest of the Rugby men. Oh, the joy if I do get it! and the disappointment if I do not. And from two of us trying at once, I fear the blow to the school would be dreadful if none of us get it. We had to work the second day as hard as on the first, on the third and fourth not so hard, nor to-day—Horace to turn into English verse, which was good for me; a divinity and mathematical paper, in which I hope my copiousness in the first made up for my scantiness in the second. Last night I dined at Magdalen, which is enough of itself to turn one's head upside down, so very magnificent. . . . I will go on now. We all assembled in the hall and had to wait an hour, the room getting fuller and fuller with Rugby Oxonians crowding in to hear the result. Every time the door opened, my heart jumped, but many times it was nothing. At last the Dean appeared in his white robes and moved up to the head of the table. He began a long preamble—that they were well satisfied with all, and that those who were disappointed were many in comparison with those who were successful, &c. All this time every one was listening with the most intense eagerness, and I almost bit my lips off till—'The successful candidates are—Mr. Stanley'—I gave a great jump, and there was a half shout amongst the Rugby men. The next was Lonsdale from Eton. The Dean then took me into the chapel, where the Master and all the Fellows were, and there I swore that I would not reveal the secrets, disobey the statutes, or dissipate the wealth of the college. I was then made to kneel on the steps and admitted to the rank of Scholar and Exhibitioner of Balliol College, 'nomine Patris, Filii, et Spiritus.' I then wrote my name, and it was finished. We start to-day in a chaise and *four* for the glory of it. You may think of my joy; the honour of Rugby is saved, and I am a scholar of Balliol!"

Dr. Arnold wrote to Mrs. Stanley :—

"I do heartily congratulate you, and heartily thank Arthur for the credit and real benefit he has conferred on us. There was a feeling abroad that we could not compete with Eton or the other great schools in the contest for University honours, and I think there was something of this even in the minds of my own pupils, however much they might value my instruction in other respects, and those who wish the school ill for my sake were ready to say that the boys were taught politics, and not taught to be scholars. Already has the effect of Arthur's success been felt here in the encouragement which it has given to others to work hard in the hope of treading in his steps, and in the confidence it has given them in my system. And yet, to say the truth, though I do think that, with God's blessing, I have been useful to your son, yet his success on this occasion is all his own, and a hundred times more gratifying than if it had been gained by my examining. For I have no doubt that he gained his scholarship chiefly by the talent and good sense of his compositions, which are, as you know, very remarkable."

Arthur Stanley remained at Rugby till the following summer, gaining more now, he considered, from Dr. Arnold than at any other time, though his uncle, Augustus Hare, who had been applied to, discouraged his being left at school so long, because, "though most boys learn most during their last year, it is when they are all shooting up together, but Arthur must be left a high tree among shrubs." Of this time are the following letters from Mrs. Stanley :—

"*February* 3, 1834.—I have just lost Arthur, and a great loss he is to me. The latter part of his time at home is always so much the most agreeable ; he gets over his reserve so much more. He has been translating and retranslating Cicero for his improvement, and has been deep in Guizot's Essay on the Civilisation of Europe, besides being chiefly engaged in a *grand* work, at present a secret, but of which you may perhaps hear more in the course of the spring. I have generally sat with him or he with me, to be ready with criticisms when wanted, and it is delightful to be so immediately and entirely understood—the why and wherefore of an objection seen before it is said. And the mind is so logical, so clear, the taste so pure in all senses, and so accurate. He goes on so quietly and perseveringly as to get through all he intends to get through without the least appearance of bustle or business. He finished his studies at home, I think, with an analysis of the Peninsular battles, trying to understand thereby the *pro* and *con* of a battle."

"*May* 21, 1834.—I have taken the opportunity of spending Sunday at Rugby. Arthur met us two miles on the road, and almost his first words were how disappointed he was that Dr. Arnold had influenza and would not be able to preach! However, I had the compensation of more of his company than under any other circumstances. There were only he and Mrs. Arnold, so that I became more acquainted with both, and altogether it was most interesting. We had the Sunday evening chapter and hymn, and it was very beautiful to see his manner to the little ones, indeed to all. Arthur was quite as happy as I was to have such an uninterrupted bit of Dr. Arnold—he talks more freely to him a great deal than he does at home."

The spring of 1834 had been saddened to the Stanleys by the death of Augustus Hare at Rome; and the decision of his widow—the beloved "Auntie" of Arthur Stanley's childhood—to make Hurstmonceaux her home, led to his being sent, for a few months before going to Oxford, as a pupil to Julius Hare, who was then Rector of Hurstmonceaux. Those who remember the enthusiastic character of Julius Hare, his energy in what he undertook, and his vigorous though lengthy elucidation of what he wished to explain, will imagine how he delighted in re-opening for Arthur

Stanley the stores of classical learning which had seemed laid aside for ever in the solitude of his Sussex living. "I cannot speak of the blessing it has been to have Arthur so long with you," his mother wrote afterwards. "He

HURSTMONCEAUX RECTORY.

says he feels his mind's horizon so enlarged, and that a foundation is laid of interest and affection for Hurstmonceaux, which he will always henceforward consider as 'one of his homes, one of the many places in the world he has to be happy in.' He writes happily from Oxford, but the lectures and sermons there do not go down after the food he has been living on at Hurstmonceaux and Rugby."

It may truly be said of Arthur Stanley that he "applied his heart to know, and to search, and to seek out wisdom." During his college life, however, his happiest days were still those rare ones which he was able to spend with the Arnolds at Rugby—his "seventh heaven," whence he wrote of spending a time of the most luxurious happiness he ever had, so unbrokenly delightful.

In this brief sketch one cannot dwell upon his happy and successful career, upon his many prizes, his honours of every kind,[1] even upon his Newdigate poem of "The Gipsies," which his father heard him deliver in the Sheldonian Theatre, and burst into tears during the tumult of applause which followed. Well remembered still is the impression produced upon the vast assembly by the beautiful lines in which the Gipsies narrate the cause of their curse :—

"They spake of lovely spots in Eastern lands,
An isle of palms, amid a waste of sands—
Of white tents pitched beside a crystal well,
Where in past days their fathers loved to dwell;

---

[1] The Ireland Scholarship and a First Class in Classics, 1837 ; the Chancellor's Latin Prize Essay, 1839 ; the English Essay, 1840, &c.

To that sweet islet came at day's decline
A Virgin Mother with her Babe Divine ;
She asked for shelter from the chill night-breeze,
She prayed for rest beneath those stately trees ;
She asked in vain—what though was blended there
A maiden's meekness with a mother's care ;
What though the light of hidden Godhead smiled
In the bright features of that blessed Child?
She asked in vain—they heard, and heeded not,
And rudely drove her from the sheltering spot.
Then fell the voice of Judgment from above,
'Who shuts Love out, shall be shut out from Love ;
Who drive the houseless wanderer from their door,
Themselves shall wander houseless evermore ;
Till He, whom now they spurn, again shall come,
Amid the clouds of heaven, to speak their final doom.'"

The suspicions which were already entertained at Oxford as to Stanley's orthodoxy
led to his being warned not to stand for Balliol,
but he was warmly welcomed to a fellowship
at University.

At Christmas, 1839, he was ordained at
St. Mary's, at Oxford, with, amongst others,
Richard Church, afterwards Dean of St. Paul's.
To the last he was full of mental difficulties
as to subscription. "If men subscribed literally to the Articles," he said, "no man in
orders, from the Archbishop to the poorest
curate on the Cumberland fells, could stay in
the Church." He was himself finally decided
by a letter from Arnold, who urged that his
own difficulties of the same kind had graduall

decreased in importance; that he had long
been persuaded that subscription to the letter
to any amount of human propositions was impossible, and that the door of ordination was
never meant to be closed against all but those
whose "dull minds and dull consciences" could
see no difficulty. Before his ordination he
wrote to his friend Vaughan :—

"Alas that a Church with so divine a service should
keep its long list of Articles! I am strengthened more
and more in my opinion that there is only needed, and
only should be, one—'I believe that Christ is both
God and man.'"

Many divines had already been shocked by
a characteristic passage which he, then still
an undergraduate, had been allowed to add to
his father's installation sermon :—

"If the heart of man be full of love and peace,
whatsoever be his outward act of division, he is not
guilty of schism. Let no man then think himself free
from schism because he is in outward conformity with
this or any other Church. He is a schismatic, and he
only, who creates feuds, scandals, and divisions in the
Church of Christ."

It was the preaching part of his clerical
duties which Arthur Stanley most dreaded.
"He could see his way to twelve sermons,

but no more." His first sermon was preached in Mr. (afterwards Bishop) Pelham's church at Bergapton. Arnold was present. The sermon was for a church building society, and the Rector had felt the subject to be a very safe one. The delivery was terrible. Mr. Somerset Hay was there. As he came out, two old women were walking very wide apart, one on one side of the road, the other on the other, to get out of the way of the carriages, and this made them raise their voices. " Mrs. Maisey," called out one of them, " how be you feeling? I got nothing. I'm very hungry." Stanley's father often spoke to him about his bad delivery.

In deciding to remain at Oxford as a tutor at University College, Stanley believed that his ordination vows might be as effectually carried out by making the most of his vocation at college, and endeavouring to influence all who came within his sphere, as by undertaking any parochial cure. To his aunt, who remonstrated, he wrote :—

" *February* 15, 1840.—I have never properly thanked you for your letters about my ordination, which I assure you, however, that I have not the less valued, and shall be no less anxious to try, as far as in me lies, to observe. It is perhaps an unfortunate thing for me,

Edward Stanley.

Bishop of Norwich.

though, as far as I see, unavoidable, that the over-
whelming considerations, immediately at the time of
ordination, were not difficulties of practice, but of subscription, and the effect has been that I would always
rather look back to what I felt to be my duty before
that cloud came on, than to the time itself. Practically,
however, I think it will in the end make no difference.
The real thing which long ago moved me to wish to go
into orders, and which, had I not gone into orders, I .
should have acted on as well as I could without orders,
was the fact that God seemed to have given me gifts
more fitting me for orders, and for that particular line
of clerical duty which I have chosen, than for any
other. It is perhaps as well to say that until I see a
calling to other clerical work, as distinct as that by
which I feel called to my present work, I should not
think it right to engage in any other; but I hope I
shall always feel, though I am afraid I cannot be too
constantly reminded, that in whatever work I am
engaged now or hereafter, my great end ought always
to be the good of the souls of others, and my great
support the good which God will give to my own soul."

Two years before this, in 1837, the Rector
of Alderley had been appointed to the Bishopric
of Norwich, and had left Cheshire amidst an
uncontrollable outburst of grief from the people
amongst whom he had lived as a friend and
a father for thirty-two years. Henceforward,
the scientific pursuits, which had occupied his
leisure hours at Alderley, were laid aside in the

no-leisure of his devotion to the See, with whose
interests he now identified his existence.   His
one object seemed to be to fit himself more
completely for dealing with ecclesiastical subjects, by gaining a clearer insight into clerical

RUIN IN THE PALACE GARDEN, NORWICH.

duties and difficulties ; and, though he long
found his diocese a bed of thorns, his kindly
spirit, his broad liberality, and all-embracing
fatherly sympathy, never failed to leave peace
behind them.   His employments were changed,

but his characteristics were the same; the geniality and simplicity shown in dealing with his clergy, and his candidates for ordination, had the same power of winning hearts which was evinced in his relation to the cottagers at

BISHOP'S BRIDGE, NORWICH.

Alderley; and the same dauntless courage which would have been such an advantage in commanding the ship he longed for in his youth, enabled him to face Chartist mobs with composure, and to read unmoved the many party censures which followed such acts as his public recognition in Norwich Cathedral of the worth of Joseph Gurney, the Quaker philanthropist; his appearance on a platform side by side with the Irish priest Father Mathew, advocating the same cause; and his enthusiastic friendship for Jenny Lind, who on his invitation made the palace her home during her stay in Norwich.

In the early years of his father's episcopate, Arthur Stanley was his father's examining chaplain for ordination candidates.   He was then a very juvenile, cherubic-looking youth. The Bishop, with characteristic hospitality, invited all the candidates to dinner.   One of them, who was not well prepared, and excessively nervous as to the result of his examination, has often narrated since how he looked round to see his dreaded future examiner. "Can you tell me which is Arthur Stanley?" he said to the bright, ingenuous-looking boy at his side.   "*Is* he here?"   And he has never forgotten the shrill voice of the youth as he said, "I am Arthur Stanley."   At first he could not believe it; then he was in a most dreadful fright.

Most delightful, and very different from the modern building which has partially replaced it, was the old Palace at Norwich.   Approached through a stately gateway, and surrounded by lawns and flowers, amid which stood a beautiful ruin—the old house with its broad old-fashioned

THE CHAPEL DOOR, PALACE, NORWICH.

staircase and vaulted kitchen, its beautiful library looking out to Mousehold and Kett's Castle, its great dining-room hung with pictures of the Christian Virtues, its picturesque and curious corners, and its quaint and intricate passages, was indescribably charming. In a little side-garden under the Cathedral, pet pee-wits and a raven were kept, which always came to the dining-room window at breakfast to be

NORWICH FROM MOUSEHOLD.

fed out of the Bishop's own hand—the only relic of his once beloved ornithological, as occa-sional happy excursions with a little nephew to Bramerton in search of fossils were the only trace left of his former geological pursuits.

" I live for my children, and for them alone I wish to live, unless in God's providence I can live to His glory," were Bishop Stanley's own words not many months before his death. He followed with longing interest the voyages of his son Owen as Commander in the *Britomart* and Captain of the *Rattlesnake*, and rejoiced in the successful career of his youngest son Charles. These were perhaps the most naturally congenial to their father, and more of companions to him when at home than any of his other children. But in the last years of his life he was even prouder of his second son Arthur, whose wonderful descriptive power and classical knowledge first became evident to his family in 1840 in his letters from Greece, which gave his intimate circle a foretaste of the interest which the outer world experienced twelve years later in the publication of " Sinai and Palestine." There were not so many travellers' letters then. " A letter from Arthur " caused the whole family to collect in the old-fashioned drawing-room at Stoke Rectory ; his aged grandparents were established in their red arm-chairs, and maps were brought out and many books of former travellers consulted, and compared with the accounts in the closely-written sheets, in which a mother's eyes easily conquered all the difficulties of the strange handwriting so often illegible to others.

Arthur Stanley's Greek tour opened a new era in his life. It was a time of limitless enjoyment—"the visions of the library at Rugby and of the lecture-room at Balliol constantly blending themselves with the visions of battles, of temples, and oracles." His enchantment came to a climax at Athens—"even more beautiful than Corfu : the long, ivy-leaf shape of the blue mountain range, the silver sea of Salamis, the hills of Pentelicus and Hymettus glowing like hot furnaces in the sun, the columns of the Parthenon and the Olympicium, with their delicate red interwoven with the deep blue sky." In describing these and similar scenes on his return, his whole being glowed and quivered with excitement.

The year 1842 was clouded by Dr. Arnold's death—"the greatest calamity," wrote Arthur Stanley, "that ever has happened to me, almost the greatest that ever can befall me." He hastened to Rugby for the following week, where he preached the funeral sermon, and he left Rugby feeling "as if he had lived years of manifold experience." "I may be thought," he wrote, "to attach an exaggerated importance to what has passed . . . but, if he was not an apostle to others, he was an apostle to me." His sorrow, his reverence, his sympathy, found relief in devoting his best energies to that " Life of Arnold," which has translated his character to the world, and given Arnold a wider influence since his death than he ever attained in his life. Perhaps, of all Stanley's books, Arnold's Life is still the one by which he is best known, and this, in his reverent love for his master, to whom he owed the building up of his mind, is as he would have wished it to be.

For twelve years Arthur Stanley resided at University College as Fellow and Tutor, undertaking also, in the latter part of the time, the laborious duties of secretary to the University Commission, into which he threw himself with characteristic ardour. In 1845 he was appointed Select Preacher to the University, an office resulting in the publication of those " Sermons and Essays on the Apostolic Age," in which he especially endeavoured to exhibit the individual human character of the different apostles.

Very comic are the recollections which Arthur Stanley's pupils retain of his lectures, which, always interesting and original, were delivered in a small voice hardly audible in the lecture-room, while the lecturer's legs were twisted round those of the table in his nervous-

ness.   He had not an idea of the usual way of
dealing with young men, or what to say to
them, least of all how to reprove them.   If one
of them was hopelessly behind-hand with some
exercise, he would meet him, and in his shyest
way say, " Good morning, Mr. Smith.   I have
. . . not had that essay, you know."   Sometimes he would rush out of his rooms to catch
the undergraduates, who would emerge from
all the corners and passages singing " For he's
a jolly good fellow," and would seize some unfortunate Bible-clerk quietly going home to his
room, instead of his real prey, and inform him,
to his astonishment, that they were going to
hold common-room upon him next morning.[1]

He was not discomfited, however, but greatly
amused, when an undergraduate told him that
the effect of his sermon in chapel the day
before had been spoilt by his having a glove
on his head the whole time.

Stanley's terribly illegible handwriting often
brought him into comical difficulties at Oxford
as elsewhere.   " Stanley never could be made
a bishop, he writes such an abominable hand,"
said Dean Wellesley.   But in printing his
books he never found this a disadvantage, as
the best readers and compositors were always

[1] Recollections of Rev. E. S. Bankes.

given to him, while the worst are bestowed on those who write best.

During this time, in which he refused the offer of Alderley Rectory, and (1849) of the Deanery of Carlisle, the recently half-empty college of University became once more crowded with students, drawn thither by his rising fame. His peculiarities did not in the least prevent his being popular. Men soon appreciated one who rejoiced in their triumphs or bewailed their disappointments as if they were his own, and who diffused into his lectures a life and geniality little known at Oxford. Meantime he had rushed, not only with ardour, but with supreme enjoyment, into the religious controversies which were exciting Oxford at the time. The publicity into which suspicions of his unorthodoxy brought his name was never without its attractions. A Church with arms wide enough to embrace almost every form and tenet of belief was already becoming his ideal of what a Christian Church should be.

The year 1849 was marked by the death of Bishop Stanley, which occurred during a visit to Brahan Castle in Scotland. Arthur was with him in his last hours, and brought his mother and sisters back to the desolate Norwich home, where a vast multitude attended the burial of the Bishop in the cathedral. "I can give you the facts," wrote one who was present, "but I can give you no notion of how impressive it was, nor how affecting. There were such sobs and tears from the school-children and from the clergy, who so loved their dear Bishop. A beautiful sunshine lit up everything, shining into the cathedral just at the time. Arthur was quite calm, and looked like an angel with a sister on each side."

From the time of his father's death, from the time when he first took his seat at family prayers in the purple chair where the venerable white head was accustomed to be seen, Arthur Stanley seemed utterly to throw off all the shyness and embarrassment which had formerly oppressed him, to rouse himself by a great effort, and henceforward to forget his own personality altogether in his position and his work. His social and conversational powers, afterwards so great, increased perceptibly from this time.

It was two days after Mrs. Stanley left Norwich that she received the news of the death of her youngest son, Charles, in Van Diemen's Land; and a very few months only elapsed before she learnt that her eldest son, Owen, had only lived to hear of the loss of his father. Henceforward his mother, saddened though not

Catherine Stanley

crushed by her triple grief, was more than ever
Arthur Stanley's care : he made her the sharer
of all his thoughts, the confidante of all his
difficulties, all that he wrote was read to her
before its publication, and her advice was not
only sought but taken.   In her new home in
London, he made her feel that she had still as
much to interest her and give a zest to life as
in the happiest days at Alderley and Norwich ;
most of all he pleased her by showing in the
publication of the " Memoir of Bishop Stanley,"
in 1850, his thorough inward appreciation of the
father with whom his outward intercourse had
been of a less intimate kind than with herself.

   In 1851 Arthur Stanley was presented to a
canonry at Canterbury, which, though he accepted it with reluctance, proved to be an
appointment entirely after his own heart,
giving him leisure to complete his " Commentary on the Corinthians," a work which,
from its deficiency in scholarship, has passed
almost unnoticed ; and leading naturally to the
" Historical Memorials of Canterbury," which,
of all his books, was perhaps the one which it
gave him most pleasure to write.   At Canterbury he not only lived amongst the illustrious
dead, but he made them rise into new life by
the way in which he spoke and wrote of them.

That he endeavoured to teach the cockatoo on its perch by the side of the paved walk leading through the canonry garden to call out "Thomas à Becket" to astonished visitors, was only typical of the way in which he interwove all the other historical recollections of the past with the daily life of the place. Often on the anniversary of Becket's murder, as the fatal hour—five o'clock on a winter's afternoon—drew near, Stanley would marshal his family and friends round the scenes of the event, stopping with thrilling effect at each spot connected with it—"Here the knights came into the cloister—here the monks knocked furiously for refuge in the church"—till, when at length the chapel of the martyrdom was reached, as the last shades of twilight gathered amid the arches, the whole scene became so real, that, with almost more than a thrill of horror, one saw the last moments through one's ears—the struggle between Fitzurse and the Archbishop, the blow of Tracy, the solemn dignity of the actual death.

Stanley had a real pride in Canterbury. In his own words, he "rejoiced that he was the servant and minister, not of some obscure fugitive establishment, for which no one cares beyond his narrow circle, but of a cathedral whose name commands respect and interest even in the remotest parts of Europe." In his inaugural lectures as professor at Oxford, in speaking of the august trophies of Ecclesiastical History in England, he said, "I need

CANON STANLEY'S HOUSE, CANTERBURY.

name but one, the most striking and obvious instance, the cradle of English Christianity, the seat of the English Primacy, *my own proud cathedral*, the metropolitan church of Canterbury."

The chief charm to Arthur Stanley of having a home of his own was that he could welcome

his mother to it, and greatly did she enjoy her
long visits to Canterbury, where she shook off
at once all the influences of her London life,
and threw herself with all her heart into the
interests of the place and its associations.
Never were the mother and son more wholly
united than in these happy years, when every
evening the literary work of the day was read
to her, and received her deepest attention,
often her severest criticism.   It was a delightful time to both, and Mrs. Stanley was one
who knew how to make the most of every
delicate shade of good in the character of her
son and daughters.   "Are not one's children
given to one," she wrote, "that we may live
over again in them when we have done living
for ourselves?"

Those who remember Stanley's happy intercourse with his mother at Canterbury; his
friendships in the place, especially with Archdeacon and Mrs. Harrison, who lived next
door, and with whom he had many daily
meetings and communications on all subjects;
his pleasure in the preparation and publication
of his "Canterbury Sermons;" his delightful
home under the shadow of the cathedral, connected by the Brick Walk with the cloisters;
and his constant work of a most congenial

kind, will hardly doubt that in many respects
the years spent at Canterbury were the most
prosperous of his life. Vividly does the recollection of those who were frequently his

SITE OF BECKET'S SHRINE, CANTERBURY.

guests go back to the afternoons when, his
cathedral duties and writing being over, he
would rush out to Harbledown, to Patrix-
bourne, or along the dreary Dover Road
(which he always insisted upon thinking most
delightful) to visit his friend Mrs. Gregory,

going faster and faster as he talked more
enthusiastically, calling up fresh topics out of
the wealthy past.   Or there were longer excursions to Bozendeane Wood, with its memories
of the strange story of the so-called Sir William
Courtenay, its blood-stained dingle amid the
hazels, its trees riddled with shot, and its wide
view over the Forest of Blean to the sea, with
the Isle of Sheppey breaking the blue waters.

Close behind Stanley's house was the Deanery and its garden, where the venerable Dean
Lyall used daily at that time to be seen walking up and down in the sun.   Here grew the
marvellous old mulberry, to preserve the life
of which, when failing, a bullock was actually
killed that the tree might drink in new life
from its blood.   A huge bough which had
been torn off from this tree had taken root,
and had become far more flourishing than its
parent.   Arthur Stanley called them the Church
of Rome and the Church of England, and gave
a lecture about it in the town.

His power of calling up past scenes of
history, painting them in words, and throwing
his whole heart into them, often enacting them,
in some respects made travelling with Arthur
Stanley delightful.   In the shorter excursions
which he made in England, those who were

with him vividly recall his intense delight in seeing the tombs of many of his intimate friends of the long ago in the cathedrals. His mother, his sister Mary, his cousin Miss Penrhyn, and his friend Hugh Pearson usually made up the summer party for longer journeys on the Continent. He was a better fellow-traveller to this familiar circle, which adored him and only went *his* way, than to any others. He was terribly impatient of being called upon to visit anything he had seen before. He hated all pictures and sculptures which were not historical. He found Dresden "the most uninteresting place he ever saw." He was quite determined never to travel with any one who "went after pictures," and he refused even to attempt acquiring any interest in art. "The difference between others and myself," he said, "breaks out in the questions we respectively ask. *They*:—'Who is the artist?' *I*:—'What is the subject?'" The *beauties* of nature had also lost in his grown-up life all the charm they had for him as a child. The scenery of Switzerland he found utterly "unmeaning," its beauties "fictitious" and dependent on clouds and sunset. In France, Spain, and Germany, a place connected with even the very smallest historic event was attractive to him, but he had no patience

with anything else.   One thing he did enjoy
everywhere.   It was tracing an often impossible
likeness between the place he was in and some
other place.   Thus his vivid fancy could imagine that Nüremberg recalled Venice ; Rheims,
Canterbury ; Amalfi, Delphi !   For several
years the family tours were confined to France
and Germany, Switzerland and Northern Italy ;
but in 1852 the Stanley group went for several
months to Italy, seeing its northern and eastern
provinces, in those happy days of *vetturino*
travelling, as they will never be seen again,
studying the story of its old towns, and eventually reaching Rome, which Mrs. Stanley had
never seen, and which her son had the greatest
delight in showing her.   It had been decided
that when the rest of the party returned to
England, he should go on to Egypt, but this
plan was changed by circumstances which
fortunately enabled him to witness the funeral
of the Duke of Wellington.   By travelling
day and night, he arrived in London the
night before the ceremony.   Almost immediately afterwards he returned to take leave of
his mother at Avignon, before starting with
his friend Theodore Walrond and two others
on that long and happy tour of which the
results have appeared in " Sinai and Pales-

tine "—rather a poetical and geographical work than a contribution to history, but a book which, without any compromise of its own freedom of thought, has turned all the knowledge of previous travellers to most admirable account. "Stanley was the most wonderful companion in the East," records one of his companions. "He got up his whole subject before, and he particularly liked to tell us everything : it fixed it in his mind. Then in the evenings he would retire to his tent, and write sheets upon sheets of those wonderful letters which only his sister could decipher and translate for other people. He had a whole mass of books with him ; one set he took with him up the Nile, and, as he came down, another met him for the Holy Land."[1]

The attention of the family was concentrated on the East in 1854, as Mary Stanley escorted a body of nurses to Constantinople, and took charge of the hospital of Koulalee during the war in the Crimea, gaining much experience at this time which was afterwards useful in her self-denying labours for the poor in London.

As his eight years at Canterbury were the happiest of Arthur Stanley's life, so for him-

[1] Recollections of Hon. T. Freemantle.

self they were the most profitable. Under
the shadow of the great cathedral he had
leisure for the literature which was the best
work of his life—not only for what he published then, but for the preparation for long
distant labours. In "that green oasis," as he
called it, he was removed from, had no calling
to, the controversies which marred his after-
life. And he lived in a peace and freedom
from abuse which at that time had its value
for him : no one cared then that he regarded
the Athanasian Creed as only a "curious
mediæval hymn."

It was in 1858 that the happy home at Canterbury was exchanged for a canonry at Christ
Church, Oxford, attached to the Professorship
of Ecclesiastical History, to which Arthur
Stanley had been appointed two years before.
His professorial appointment had not been
welcomed at first, and he used to say that a
letter from Jowett was the only letter of con-
gratulation he received upon it. But his
three "Introductory Lectures on the Study of
Ecclesiastical History," delivered before his
residence, had attracted such audiences as have
seldom been seen in the University Theatre,
and aroused an enthusiasm which was the
greatest encouragement to him in entering

upon a course of life so different from that
he had left ; for he saw how a set of lectures
usually wearisome could be rendered interesting to all his hearers, how he could make the
dry bones live.

Henceforward, for some years, the greater
portion of Stanley's days was spent in his
pleasant study on the ground floor (in the
first house on the left after entering Peck-
water from Tom quad), looking upon his little
walled garden, with its miniature lawn and
apple-trees, between which he was delighted
to find that he could make a fountain ; attended
to by his faithful married butler and house-
keeper ; concerning whom, when some one
remarked disparagingly upon their increasing
family, he is recollected characteristically to
have exclaimed, "I do not know if they will
have many children, but I do know one thing,
that, if they have a hundred, I shall never
part with Mr. and Mrs. Waters."

Here he was always to be found standing
at his desk, tossing off sheet after sheet, the
whole floor covered with scraps of papers
written or letters received, which, by a habit
that nothing could change, he generally tore
up and scattered around him. Here were composed those Lectures on the Eastern, and after-

E

wards on the Jewish Church, to which Stanley's
"picturesque sensibility," as Lord Beaconsfield
called it, so exactly fitted him to do justice
—Lectures which have done more than anything ever written to make the Bible history
a living reality instead of a dead letter, which,
while with the freedom which excited such an
outcry against Dean Milman, they do not scruple
to describe Abraham as a Chaldean Sheykh
of the desert, Rachel as a Bedouin chief's
daughter, and Joseph as the royal officers are
exhibited in the Theban sculptures, open such
a blaze of sunshine upon those venerable histories, that those who look upon them by the
new light feel as if they had never seen them
before.

Stanley liked excessively the importance of
his new position at Oxford. "There is a
pleasure," he wrote, "in finding oneself at the
top of a tree ; everything open to one's view,
great persons civil, smaller persons grateful
for notice." It was also a great enjoyment to
him in the years of his Oxford life to take
up the threads of many old friendships which
years of separation had relaxed. He observed
with some dismay how the intellectual power of
the University had ceased to take orders. But
he took advantage of introductions from Rugby,

and of the acquaintances made in college by a young cousin residing in his house, to invite many undergraduates to his Canonry, by seeing them again and again to become intimate with

CANON STANLEY'S HOUSE, CHRIST CHURCH.

them, and in many cases to gain a permanent influence over them. His conversation was considered versatile rather than accurate, brilliant rather than profound. But those he was really at home with, will always retain a

delightful recollection of the home-like evenings
in his pleasant drawing-room, of his sometimes
reading aloud, of his fun and playfulness, and of
his talking over his future lectures and getting
his younger companions to help him with draw-
ings and plans for them. The very childlike
helplessness of the Canon had its attraction to
those who were much with him and loved him.
But it has been rightly said that "he went
dreamily about the world, puzzled and put out
by its every-day requirements, always demand-
ing some one to take care of him, and generally
finding what he sought." Upon the University
Stanley never made any deep impression, whilst
he obtained an influence over a great many
individuals. The Prince of Wales, then an
undergraduate, was frequently at his house, and
many more visitors from the outside world came
to the Canonry at Oxford than to that at Canterbury — Germans, Americans, and the friends
Stanley had made during a tour in Russia.

An article which Arthur Stanley contributed
in 1861 to the *Edinburgh Review* in defence of
the authors of "Essays and Reviews" would
have destroyed all hopes of a bishopric, if he
had wished for it. To his mother, who felt
how utterly he was unsuited to episcopal life,
this was an unmixed cause for rejoicing. "If it

had rained mitres as thick as hail," said Jowett,
" Stanley had such a curiously shaped head that
they would never have fitted it."

In the early spring of 1862, in fulfilment of a
wish which had been expressed by the Prince
Consort, Arthur Stanley was desired to accom-
pany the Prince of Wales in his projected tour to
the East.   In looking forward to this journey,
he chiefly considered with joy how he might
turn the travel to the best account for his royal
companion, and how he might open for his
service the stores of information which he had
laid up during his former Eastern tour.   But
he combined the duties of chaplain with those
of cicerone, and his sermons preached before
the Prince of Wales at Tiberias, Nazareth, and
other holy sites of sacred history were afterwards published in a small volume.   " Gather
up the fragments that remain, that nothing be
lost," was his constant teaching in Palestine.
" It is by thinking of what has been here, by
making the most of things we see in order to
bring before our minds the things we do not
see, that a visit to the Holy Land becomes a
really religious lesson."   To Stanley's delight,
one great event marked the royal tour in the
East : the Mosque of Hebron, hitherto inexor-
ably closed, was thrown open to the travellers.

It had not been without many sad and
anxious misgivings that Stanley had consented
to obey the desire, not command, of his Queen,
in being a second time separated from his
mother for so long a time and by so great a
distance.   He never saw her again, yet he was
the only one of her children who received her
farewell words, and embrace, and blessings.   A
few days after he was gone she became ill, and
on the morning of the 5th of March, in pain-
less unconsciousness, she died.   It was as well,
perhaps, that the dear absent son was not
there, that he had the interest of a constant
duty to rouse him.   He returned in June.
Terrible indeed is the recollection of the piteous
glance he cast towards his mother's vacant
corner, and mournfully, to those who were
present, did the thought occur, *what* it would
have been if she had been there then, especially
then, with the thousand things there were to
tell her.   " Nothing," he said, " can ever make
my mother's memory other than the greatest
gift I have received."

Sad indeed were the months which followed,
till, in the autumn of 1863, Arthur Stanley was
appointed to the Deanery at Westminster—
"the one change," he wrote, "that my dearest
mother desired for me."   This was soon fol-

lowed by the fulfilment of a still dearer wish of hers for him, and sunshine again flowed in upon his life with his marriage, in Westminster Abbey, to Lady Augusta Bruce, fifth daughter of the seventh Earl of Elgin, whom he had first met at the house of Madame Mohl in 1857.

Of all that his marriage was to Dean Stanley it is impossible to speak—of his true and perfect companionship with Lady Augusta, of the absolute completeness with which she filled the position of his wife, of mistress of the Deanery, of leader of every good work in Westminster, where her goodness, wisdom, and tact were always in evidence and won all hearts. She loved the poor. She had an ennobling influence upon all. There were those who cavilled at the universal cordiality of her manner, but, as they knew her better, they learnt that it was an echo from her heart. "By her supporting love he was comforted for his mother's death, and her character, though cast in another mould, remained to him, with that of his mother, the brightest and most sacred vision of earthly experience."

Going soon after his marriage to visit Hugh Pearson at Sonning, he went on the box of the fly. "I see you've got Lady Augusta Bruce inside," said the driver; "I remember her very

well at Windsor."—"Not Lady Augusta *Bruce*
—she is Lady Augusta Stanley now—she is
my wife."—"Well then I *do* wish you joy, for
your wife is just the best woman in England."
Highly delighted was the Dean with this.

Congenial, as all Stanley's other homes,
were the surroundings of the residence under
the walls of the Abbey, decorated by much of
the old oak furniture, inanimate friends, which
had already travelled from Alderley to Norwich,
Canterbury, and Oxford.   Most delightful was
the library at the Deanery, a long room surrounded by bookcases, with a great gothic
window at the end, and a curious picture of
Queen Elizabeth let in above the fireplace.
Here, all through the mornings, in which
visitors, with very rare exceptions, were never
admitted, the Dean stood at his desk and
scattered his papers as of old, while Lady
Augusta employed herself at her writing-table
close by.   His "Memorials of Westminster,"
full of attractive glimpses of history ; the second
and third volume of his "Jewish Church," which
he considered to be the best contribution he
could make to the religious changes of the time,
and into the graphic picturesqueness of which
he threw all the vigour of his early writings ;
his "Address on the Three Irish Churches,"

characteristically advocating the equal endow-
ment, under State management, of the Protes-

COURTYARD, DEANERY, WESTMINSTER.

tant Episcopalian, Roman Catholic, and Presby-
terian Churches; his "Lectures on the Church of
Scotland," in which, through a brilliant review of

the ecclesiastical story of Scotland, he claims
the highest distinction for the Established
Church ; his Addresses as Lord Rector of St.
Andrews, and many articles for the *Quarterly*,
the *Edinburgh*, the *Nineteenth Century*, *Good
Words*, and *Macmillan's Magazine*, flowed
from his pen in this room ; and lastly, his
" Christian Institutions," which seem written
chiefly to disabuse people of the fancy of Roman
Catholic and High Church divines, that they
can discover in the Early Church their own
theories concerning the Papacy, the hierarchy,
and the administration of the Sacraments.   It
was a necessity to Stanley to be always writing
something, and the same passion for impossible
analogies appeared in all he wrote.   He often
latterly returned to the pursuit of his earliest
days, and expressed himself in verse, but he
wrote nothing thus that will live.

More than ever did friends gather around
Stanley during his life at the Deanery, as much
as ever was he able to enjoy the pleasures of
society, growing every year more full of anec-
dote, of animation, of interesting recollections.
And the visitors whom the Dean and Lady
Augusta delighted to receive comprised every
class of society, from their royal mistress and
her children to great bands of working-men,

whom it was an especial pleasure to Arthur Stanley to escort over the Abbey himself, picking out and explaining the monuments most interesting to them. Every phase of opinion, every variety of religious belief, above all, those who most widely differed from their host, were cordially welcomed in the hospitalities of the Deanery ; and the circle which gathered in its drawing-rooms, especially on Sunday evenings after the service in the Abbey, was singularly characteristic and unique. Amid these, "small, swift, rapid, almost precipitate in his movements," the little eager Dean moved constantly, his thoughts on the history of the time, in which, in the vivid pictures of his imagination, he was always one of the most conspicuous actors, overflowing in a torrent of words at once harmonious and pictorial.

He always spoke more of events or of scenes than of politics—perhaps because, as to the latter, he was a little uncertain of himself; for while in his personal politics he adored Gladstone, the sunshine of court favour always made him appear to sympathise with Lord Beaconsfield. "When disposed to be friendly," says Dean Church, "Stanley was very delightful and attractive ; and I think what made him so was not his brilliancy and resource and knowledge, but the sense that he was sincerely longing to be in sympathy with every one for whom he could feel respect. Yet he had a certain freely indulged contempt for what he did not like, and a disposition to hunt down and find faults when he did not love people." Most cordially did Lady Augusta unite with the Dean in wishing that the spare rooms of the house should be ceaselessly filled with a succession of guests, to meet whom the most appropriate parties were always invited, or who were urged by the Dean unrestrainedly to invite their own friends, especially the now aged " Auntie," his mother's sister, long the survivor, as he expressed it, " of a blessed brotherhood and sisterhood."

Greater, too, than the interest of all his other homes was that which Stanley found in the Abbey of Westminster—" the royal and national sanctuary which has for centuries enshrined the manifold glories of the kingdom "—of which he had become the natural guardian and caretaker. There are those who have smiled at the eagerness he occasionally displayed to obtain the burial of an illustrious person in the Abbey against all opposition. There are those who have been incapable of understanding his anxiety to guard and keep the Abbey as it had been delivered to him; wisely objecting even

to give uniformity to a rudely patched pavement,
on account of the picturesqueness and the
human interest attached to its variations of
colour and surface ; delighting in the characteristics of his choir projecting into the nave, like
the *coro* of a Spanish cathedral ;[1] carefully,
even fiercely, repelling any attempt to show
more deference to the existing monuments
of one age than of another, each being a
portion of history in itself, and each, when
once placed there, having become a portion
of the history of the Abbey, never to be dis-
placed. The Abbey became dearer to him
than any other building in the world. He
gave fresh life to it. He restored the beautiful
Chapter House, which had been used as a
Record Office. He brought together again the
fragments of Torrigiani's altar, which served
as a tomb to Edward VI. He removed
Catherine de Valois from the vault of the
Percies to rest by her husband Henry V.

---

[1] It was painful to those who knew the Dean well to see a letter in
the *Times* a few days after his death, urging that the destruction of the
choir—the thing of all others he most deprecated—should be carried
out as a memorial of him ! Those who wish to know what he really
desired for his Abbey have only to read the preface to his " Memorials
of Westminster," expressing his anxious suggestion of a cloister for the
reception of future monuments, enclosing the Jewel Tower, on the
present site of Abingdon Street, to face the Palace of Westminster on
one side, and the College Garden on the other.

His care in collecting and replacing the
fragments of the reredos of St. Michael's
altar, and his curious amalgamation of tiny
fragments of lost screens and altars in the
Chapter House, are marks of his tender care
for the minutest details of the Abbey, which
it was his great object to preserve, to enrich,
but never, under any false pretext of "restoration" or improvement, to change.   How enraptured he was to discover the monogram of
Izaak Walton scratched by the angler himself upon the tomb of Isaac Casaubon ; how
delighted to describe the funeral of Henry V.,
in which his three chargers were led up
to the altar as mourners behind his waxen
effigy ; how enchanted to make any smallest
discovery with regard to those to whom the
more obscure monuments are erected, to trace
out the whole history of " Jane Lister, dear
childe," who is buried in the cloisters, and
upon whom he preached one of his sermons
to children ; how pleased to answer some one
who cavilled at the space allotted to the
monument of Mrs. Grace Gethin, with the
quotations referring to her in Congreve and
D'Israeli.   One of his last thoughts connected
with outside life was the erection of a monument to mark "the common pit" into which the

remains of the family and friends of the great Protector were thrown at the Restoration.

At Westminster Stanley preached more often than he had ever done before ; but two classes of his sermons there will be especially remembered — those on Innocents' Day to children, so particularly congenial to one whose character had always been so essentially that of the "pure in heart," and those on the deaths of illustrious Englishmen—*oraisons funèbres* —often preached in the Abbey, even when those commemorated were not to repose there. "He had," said Dr. Stoughton, "a felicitous, perhaps over-taxed, gift of adapting passages of Scripture to passing events." "Charity, Liberality, Toleration," these became more than ever the watchwords of his teaching, of his efforts to inculcate the spirit that would treat all who follow Christ as brothers, by whatever path they might be approaching Him, and by whatever hedges they might be divided. Those who heard him will always remember the eagerness of "the little figure with the sweet, refined, earnest face on these occasions." His last utterance in the Abbey, on Saturday, July 9, 1881, was on the text "Blessed are the merciful, for they shall obtain mercy. Blessed are the pure in heart, for they shall

see God,"—one of his course of sermons on
the Beatitudes.   In everything his precept
was that of the aged St. John—"Little children, love one another."

It was with the fancy that in life, as in
death, he could make the Abbey the great
temple of conciliation, that the most hetero-
geneous preachers were invited by Arthur
Stanley to make use of its pulpit—preachers
from the very north and south and east and
west of religious opinion.   His delight in con-
tradictions, which made him ask guests of
the most opposite opinions to meet at his
table, came out even more in his decanal
office.   A catholic, comprehensive, all-embracing Christianity was what he sought; though
to many it seemed as if his main object
must be to bring into the Abbey those who
had no right to be there.   Max Müller, a lay-
man; Caird and Tulloch, Nonconformists; Archdeacon Reichel, Dr. Stoughton, Dr. Moffat, and
even Dr. Colenso, were amongst those invited to preach; and he showed an innate
and mysterious sympathy with heretics of
every kind.   Only from the High Churchmen
did he receive refusals.   Pusey declined to
preach in the Abbey because the Dean had
endorsed Colenso's book, so "frightfully un-

settling to the faith of the lower classes : "
Liddon, who afterwards consented, refused at
first because he could not preach in a pulpit
which had been contaminated by Maurice :
Keble, because he would not seem to "bear
with doctrines" which Stanley avowedly up-
held.

It has been asserted, perhaps justly, that Stanley went so far in his efforts for comprehensive-
ness (*i.e.* charity) that he did away with the
ordinary meanings of terms.   As Donald Mac-
leod has said—"'Latitudinarian,' with most
opprobrious sense, was the epithet hurled at
him, but 'Latitudinarian,' in the better signi-
ficance of wide toleration, was the title he
would himself have gloried in."   The controversies into which he remorselessly plunged
himself were felt, by all his best friends, to—
not sour, but somewhat embitter his character,
to impair his usefulness, and mar his influence,
as well as to waste his time, so ephemeral and
unimportant was their nature.   But his love
of controversy seemed like a passion, leading
him to espouse the cause of heretics in whatever form they might exist.   It made his
career at Westminster, what Jowett described
it, "brilliant but melancholy."   What his own
exact faith was, no one knew when he was

alive, no one has been able to make out since. That it was highly inappropriate to a Dean of Westminster is the only fact that is quite certain. He certainly disbelieved, on historic grounds, all the Biblical miracles except the Resurrection, and the expression " Jesus is the Son of God " was used by him in no doctrinal sense, but only as a summary of the life and character of our most holy example. And yet he ever maintained that the greatest of all miracles was the character of Christ; it was for the Christlike side of all Churches and all Christians that he endeavoured to testify his appreciation, and he did this so fully that Maurice said, " Stanley has done more to make the Bible a living reality in the homes of the people than any living writer ; " and the Bishop of Manchester, that Stanley daily brought down light from heaven into the lives of other people.

Possibly his most definite confession of a mildewed faith was given in his sermon on the death of Kingsley, when, after insisting that the main part of the religion of mankind and of Christendom should consist in the strict fulfilment of the duty of man, which is the will of God, he says, " The first and last business of every living being, whatever his station, party, creed, tastes, desires, is Morality. Virtue, virtue, always virtue." Or perhaps a fuller profession of faith is found in his lines on the Ascension :—

> "He is gone : towards their goal
> World and Church must onward roll.
> Far behind we leave the past ;
> Forward are our glances cast.
>
> Still His words before us range
> Through the ages as they change.
> Wheresoe'er the Truth shall lead,
> He will give whate'er we need."

It is mentioned as amusingly characteristic of Stanley that when the Greek Archbishop of Syra was taking part in a consecration in the Abbey, he should say, whilst inveighing against the damnatory clauses, "It is interesting to remember that this excellent person, not holding the Double Procession of the Holy Ghost according to the Athanasian Creed, *without doubt* shall perish everlastingly."

That abuse should be abundantly showered upon "the heretic Dean" was not unnatural, and greatly did he enjoy it. It came from the most diverse quarters and was made for the most diverse reasons, but his love of warfare and a struggle made it a positive delight to him. It has been truly said, especially with reference to his life at Westminster, that "War was in

his heart, while Peace was on his lips." When
he permitted a new reredos with statues of
saints to be erected in the Abbey, he received
a letter beginning, ".Thou miserable idolater."
And he left behind him a whole parcel of
letters of the most scurrilous abuse, labelled—
" May God forgive the writers as I do."

The thought of the Abbey recalls the Jeru-
salem Chamber and the meetings within its
walls of the Lower House of Convocation, in
which the Dean so frequently spoke, and often
perhaps in too vehement defence of a cause
or a person he thought to be unjustly oppressed, often perhaps incurring the silent
censure of many a remote country parsonage
by the expression of his opinions, but ever
with kindly feelings towards those from whom
he differed the most, and who, when they
knew him well, seldom failed to love and
appreciate him. Through life the exemplifi-
cation of Christian catholicity in his own
person, Stanley could hardly help taking part
with those who were attacked, whenever he
saw that religious animosity was excited.
"Charity suffereth long and is kind" was
never absent from his thoughts, and led him
to be ever the champion of those whom he
imagined to be persecuted, as much of the

writers in " Essays and Reviews," of Bishop
Colenso, Père Hyacinthe, and even of Mr.
Voysey, as of the Tractarians in early life.
Yet to many it seemed a strange inconsistency
that, while he did not scruple publicly to sub-
scribe for the defence of Mr. Voysey, he should
refuse the use of the Abbey to the Archbishop
of Canterbury for the special service before the
Pan-Anglican Synod.   Thus it naturally came
about, as Dean Church says, that "his influence was a very mixed one, depressing as
well as elevating, raising the standard of religious ideas and work, but also confusing and
thwarting very much in detail."   His inmost
heart meanwhile was bent upon the ennobling
and purifying of his fellow-men.   "If together
we cannot do something for London, may the
malison of St. Peter and St. Paul be upon
us," he wrote to the Dean of St. Paul's on
his appointment in 1871.   But it was not as
a Churchman, but as a literary man of extra-
ordinarily picturesque charm and personality
that he never failed to have a fascinating
and elevating influence upon all who came in
contact with him.

Next to the immediate concerns of his
Abbey, what occupied Stanley was the welfare
of the poor around him, whom he tried without

ceasing to raise, cheer, and enliven, sending
many a mental sunbeam into a dismal home
by the thought of his annual flower-show and
its prizes, and taking great personal interest
in the neighbouring hospital and its work.
In all his efforts for the people of Westminster, the Dean was ably seconded by
Lady Augusta.   His desire to benefit the
working classes was also shared by his elder
sister, Mary, who, in a direction quite inde-
pendent of his own, was unceasingly employed
in trying to find employment for the poor, to
teach them provident habits, and to improve
their homes.   At one time she undertook the
anxiety of a large contract to supply the army
with shirts, in order to give employment to a
great number of poor women.   Latterly her
wonderful powers of organisation always enabled her to deal with vast numbers, but it
had taken long years of personal work amongst
the people to acquire her experience, as well
as the respect and confidence which contributed so much to the success of her schemes
for their good.   Of all these, the most important was the Penny Bank, opened once a
week in a little court at the back of a house
in York Street, Westminster, and managed
personally by Miss Stanley for more than

twenty-five years, though it had as many as
1000 depositors at a time. The undertaking
was indescribably laborious, especially during
the annual audit week in December, when
every single account had to be compared with
that in the ledger. In itself this ledger was
a study—the dates for the whole half year
on one page (to save turning over), the
blotting-paper stitched in between each leaf
(to save blotting), for in dealing with such
large numbers every instant of time saved
was of importance. No less remarkable was
the simple but ingenious device by which the
visits of her numerous clients were distributed
equally over the three hours that she sat at
the receipt of custom, so that each should be
speedily served, and that there should be no
undue crowding at one time. Mary Stanley
would invite four or five ladies, before the
people arrived, to come and tie up flowers
for them in bunches. Many hundreds of nose-
gays were thus prepared, and it is remembered
how anxious she was that they should be
prettily arranged, for "I want to give my
people what is beautiful, and what is worth
doing at all is worth doing *well.*" Her in-
variable patience, quickness, and good-humour
with the people rendered what would have

*

been impossible to many comparatively easy to Mary Stanley; but a brave heart was also required, and a friend who thought of starting a similar bank in another part of London, and came to her with all its dangers and difficulties, recalls the energy with which she closed the discussion : " My dear, if you stand counting the difficulties when there is a good work before you, you will never do anything that is worth doing all your life! Only begin, begin, begin, and the difficulties will all disappear." Under other superintendence and in another house the Penny Bank founded by Mary Stanley still flourishes in Westminster, a memorial of her energy, kindliness, and wisdom.

As Dean of Westminster Stanley still enjoyed in summer many foreign tours, when the pleasure of showing places to Lady Augusta sometimes counterbalanced his hatred of revisiting what he had seen before. In these tours he visited Vallombrosa, Canosa, Gergovia, Sedan, and many other historic sites; he made the acquaintance of Nardi, Dupanloup, D'Aubigné; he attended the Old Catholic Congress at Munich and Cologne; he had a quaint interview with Pius IX., and he became the intimate friend of Père Hyacinthe. " There is nothing in the world," he wrote, " that in-

terests me so much as an ecclesiastical curiosity." He had still the most thorough
enjoyment in travelling—" It tires one out in
body, but is a most unspeakable refreshment
in mind." Meantime historic events of his
own time thrilled him with interest. He
bitterly regretted the "fall of the Papacy, as
involving the destruction of a quaint historical
anomaly." "My great wish in this life," he
said, "is to be Pope. Then I would call a
General Council, and I should say, 'Am I
infallible?'—'Yes.'—'Is whatever I say certain
to be true?'—'Yes.'—'Then the first use I
make of my infallibility is to declare I am
not infallible, that no Pope ever was infallible,
that the Church has fallen into many grievous
errors, and stands in great need of refor-
mation."

Dean Stanley's marriage with the devoted
attendant of the Duchess of Kent, whom the
Queen honoured with unvaried kindness and
friendship, had brought him into constant
communication with the Court, to which the
outward tie had been drawn closer by his
appointment of Deputy Clerk of the Closet,
Chaplain to the Queen, and Chaplain to the
Prince of Wales. He was summoned every
year to take part in the services which com-

memorate at Frogmore the death of the
beloved Prince Consort. It was after repre-
senting her royal mistress at the marriage of

CHANTRY OF HENRY V., WESTMINSTER.

the Duke of Edinburgh in the bitter Russian
cold of January 1874, that Lady Augusta
Stanley received the chill from which she
never recovered. Amid the heartrending

sorrow of watching her gradual failure of every power, her being obliged to lay aside one duty or pleasure after another, the news that he had been elected Lord Rector of St. Andrews brought a temporary sunbeam to Arthur Stanley. The duties of the appointment were just what, at a happier time, he would most have enjoyed, and he did enjoy giving his inaugural lecture, and describing that "secluded sanctuary of ancient wisdom, with the foam-flakes of the Northern ocean driving through its streets, with the skeleton of its antique magnificence lifting up its gaunt arms into the sky."

But Lady Augusta continued to fail daily. For nearly a year longer her visible presence was still with him, a year of hopes and fears, a year of sad forebodings and farewells, and on Ash Wednesday, 1876, one of the happiest of earthly unions was severed by her death at Westminster. On her deathbed she said, "Think of me as near, only in another room —in my Father's house are many mansions." But

> "The sunshine of the heart was dead,
> The glory of the home was fled,
> The smile that made the dark world bright,
> The love that made all duty light."

For five years Arthur Stanley was left to

fulfil his appointed task alone.   After a time he
was full of animation still, his mental activity
was as great as ever, and he was always full of
work.   He found much interest in a short tour
in the United States, where, he said, he was
chiefly struck by his own ignorance ; and after
that by the extraordinary difference between
the States — like separate kingdoms.   The
kindly welcome and friendship shown him in
America seemed, at the time, almost to make
him happy.   Sometimes also in England, when
he was in the society of those whose thoughts
met his, some of his old animation and cheer-
fulness returned ; and he ever gratefully recog-
nised and reciprocated the loving attention with
which his home was cared for by his wife's
sister, and her cousin who had been more than
a sister.   But his friends saw him change more
and more every year—his hair became grey,
his figure became bent, his voice became feeble ;
and, after the death of his dear sister Mary, in
the autumn of 1879, had loosened another of
his closest ties to earth, he seemed to be only
waiting for a summons which could not be very
far off.   In speaking of what he would do in
the future, he now always said, " If I am still
here," and he looked at places he had loved as
if for the last time.

On Good Friday, 1881, he preached upon the words, "Father, into Thy hands I commend my spirit." He said he had preached the same sermon in the same pulpit at that season ten years before, and he would like to preach it once again. The way in which he said "once again" sent a thrill of sadness through all who heard it.

On Saturday, July 9, during one of his sermons on the Beatitudes, he was taken ill in the Abbey, and though there were few who believed him in danger till within some hours of the end, all through the week which followed he was being led gently and painlessly to the entrance of the dark valley, and on July 18, just before the Abbey clock struck the hour of midnight, surrounded by almost all those he most loved on earth, his spirit passed away. His sister, who sat constantly by his side through the last hours, wrote afterwards :—

"There he lay, immovable and speechless, only just breathing heavily.

"As we gathered round his bed, the deep silence was only broken by a few prayers offered up at intervals by Canon Farrar and my husband. Then, for the last half-hour, as the breathing became fainter, the silence grew more intense. No one stirred or spoke, only the nurse went on fanning his dear face as the shadows

of death grew darker.   At length even the fan ceased,
and there was stillness absolutely uninterrupted.

"A long pause—another faint breath—a pause yet
longer—again a breath fainter than the last.   Another
long, long pause, and when for some moments we had
waited for another breath which never came, we knew
that he had left us, and we knelt down and offered up
our thanks for the peaceful departure of our dear, dear
brother.   And so we came away, as the cathedral
chimes struck a quarter to twelve, and left that room,
never to meet there again for ever."

He was buried with immense concourse of
people—one might almost say with the great
pomp which he loved—and rests by Lady
Augusta's side in Henry VII.'s chapel at Westminster ; but his funeral was far less touching
and impressive than hers, for he was not there
to be felt for and sorrowed with.

In speaking of his dear Westminster, the
sense of the Dean's last words was, " I have
laboured amidst many frailties and with much
weakness to make this institution more and
more the great centre of religious and national
life in a truly liberal spirit."

This was the characteristic of his existence ;
thus—since he has passed beyond all bounds of
doubt or controversy—in most loving reverence
should he ever be remembered.

HENRY ALFORD

I HAVE been asked to write some memorial of my dear friend Dean Alford. The remembrance of his strong personality is ever present with me. I can hear his genial voice still, and feel myself carried away by his enthusiasm for all things good and beautiful ; and yet, in gathering up the fragments that remain, there is not much to be told. He was one of those who always poured out his best thoughts in books, not in his letters, which are neither graphic nor characteristic. Of his published works there is a perfect library. Outside them, he had only his personal existence, infinitely loving and lovable ; replete with tenderest care for others and utter indifference about himself; full of little peculiarities, which, to those who loved him, had their own charm as being his. What chiefly strikes one on looking back is, that no one had a more vigorous sense of enjoyment than Dean Alford, or more power of diffusing it ; whether in the old Deanery, under the shadow of his own glorious cathedral, or in thymy uplands of the Roman Campagna, or amid the grand purple precipices of the Maritime Alps, his companions were equally carried away by it.

Henry Alford was born in London on October 7, 1810, being the son of the Rev. Henry Alford and his wife, Sarah Eliza Paget (daughter of a Tamworth banker), who died four months after the birth of her only child. His earliest amusement was to write books, and he became the author of " The Travels of St. Paul, from his Conversion to his Death "— illustrated—at six years old.

As curate of Steeple Ashton in Wiltshire, and afterwards of Wraxall near Bristol, his father was his constant companion and friend. Henry Alford portrays their intimate relationship in the " School of the Heart "—

> " Evening and Morning—those two ancient names
> So link'd with childish wonder, when with arms
> Fast wound about the neck of one beloved,
> Oft questioning, we heard Creation's tale,—
> Evening and Morning brought to me strange joy."

In 1817 the father went abroad with Lord Calthorpe, and Henry, at seven years old, was sent to school at Charmouth. After returning to England in 1818, his father took the curacy of Drayton, which was only a mile from Heale

House in Somerset, where his elder brother, Samuel, lived with his numerous children, who were like brothers and sisters to the little Henry.

In 1824 Henry Alford was sent to Ilminster School—a gentle, delicate boy, with wondrous powers of memory, of unusually serious thoughts, which found minute expression in the self-examination of his journal, or in letters of meditative piety and advice addressed to his cousins at Heale. His school companions never lost the impression that he was a genius, with a natural talent for everything. "His mind was always poetical and imaginative, loving scenery, flowers, and whatever constituted beauty in nature and art. He was humorous and witty, with a quick sense of whatever was ludicrous and amusing, and was ready to get pleasure out of the least thing." Above all, his school companions always retained the impression of the extraordinary purity of his boyish life. One of them well remembers his saying in early years, when speaking of the titles given to our Saviour, that he liked to call him " Jesus, my Master." [1]

In the summer of 1827, Henry Alford left Ilminster to go to a tutor at Acton in Suffolk. This tutor was the Rev. John Bickersteth, under

---

[1] Letter from America. Memoir, p. 492.

G

whose influence his religious tendencies deve-
loped.   On November 18, 1827, he wrote in a
Bible, " I do this day, as in the presence of God
and my own soul, renew my covenant with God,
and solemnly determine henceforth to become
His, and to do His work as far as in me lies."
As the time of going to Cambridge approached,
he trembled before the temptations which were
sure there to assail him.   To one of his cousins
he wrote :—

"You cannot think how I dread Cambridge ; I quite
shrink from the thought of going there, and fear I shall
fall.   I have no stamina as yet of religious principle,
at least so I fear, and all as yet is talk and pride.
People want me to get into the first class at Trinity.
I hope I shall be enabled to do my best as in the sight
of God, and not to regard the praise or dispraise of
men, and then, if I fail of my object of attainment of
earthly honours, I can be calm and contented under
the will of my Heavenly Father."

Settled at Trinity, he was soon deep in lectures and enjoying all his classical studies, but
finding nothing " satisfying" except the Bible.

"I read Æschylus and Homer," he says, "and then
turn to Isaiah and Joel; and the heathen poetry,
sublime as it is in itself, is mere prose in comparison.
I read Algebra and Euclid, and then turn to the
Epistle to the Romans, and all the reasoning of ancients

and moderns appears weak and inconclusive; every
store of spiritual and intellectual knowledge is hid in
that divine book."

His letters lack the simplicity of youth, and
are full of moral reflections.   After apologising
for this in a letter to his cousin, Fanny Alford
(June 16, 1829), he says :—

"I cannot help it.   It seems natural to my mind to
think on things which are going on around me, as if
they carried an instruction with them, and were meant
in some measure to bear a secondary meaning, and teach
a lesson of spirituality and heavenly-mindedness."

To Walter Alford he wrote from Cambridge
in the following October :—

"It is not so much the gross outward temptations of
this or any other place that I have to fear; my inmost
feelings recoil and turn with disgust from the brutality
and sensuality of many men whom I see around;
but it is the insidious undermining, if I may say so,
which study and literary habits carry on against the
work of God in the soul; it is the springing up of those
seeds of pride which an enemy hath sown in my heart,
and which are working slowly, but I fear surely, towards
maturity—the pride of intellectual, philosophical, or
classical acquirements—it is these I have to dread.   Oh,
the chilling influence of literary pursuits and literary
society!"

He wrote also of the temptations which he felt from "being constantly brought into contact with men who live without God in the world, and in being surrounded with professors of religion, many of them neither moral nor religious."

In leisure moments, Henry Alford often occupied himself in translating favourite passages in the classics for his cousins, and urging them to compare them with still nobler passages in the Scriptures. " You cannot think how beautiful it is," he wrote, " to select and admire the sublimest and finest parts of the classical philosophers and poets, and then to find parallel passages in Scripture, as may almost always be done, and comparing them ; not to destroy the beauty of the former, but to exalt and bring into light the divine sublimity of the latter."

His chief college friendships seem to have been with Arthur Hallam, Tennant, and Alfred Tennyson. Writing of Alford's college life, Dean Merivale says :—

"I really think he was morally the bravest man I ever knew. His perfect purity of mind and singleness of purpose, seemed to give him a confidence and unobtrusive self-respect which never failed him. Then, as throughout his career, he was singularly remarkable for the versatility of his talents. If one of the friends

among whom he was then held in estimation was more
eminently gifted in verse, another more deeply plunged
into the dark profound of juvenile metaphysics, a third
promising to take higher rank in classics, a fourth in
mathematics, Alford could at least hold his own with
all of them, could appreciate all, could sympathise with
all, and could gain in return the sympathy of all."

In 1831 Henry Alford's habits of self-examination increased to what many would feel
to be a very unwholesome extent. In the
words of Bishop Beveridge he wrote, "My
very repentance wants repenting of ; my holiest
acts want purifying afresh in the blood of
Christ."

> "Even the Love of Him
> Now mingled in my bosom with all sounds
> And sights that I rejoiced in—and in hours
> Of self-arraigning thought, when the dull world,
> With all its saws of heartlessness and pride,
> Came close upon me, I approved my joys
> And simple fondnesses, on trust that He
> Who taught the lesson of unwavering faith
> From the meek lilies of green Palestine,
> Would fit the earthly things that most I loved
> To the high teaching of my patient soul.
> And the sweet hope that sprung within me now
> Seemed all-capacious, and from every source
> Apt to draw comfort."[1]

Meantime he worked tremendously hard.
"In those days he almost seemed to do with-

[1] From "The School of the Heart."

out sleep," wrote one of his intimate friends
and companions.   In January 1832 he was announced thirty-fourth wrangler, eighth in the
first class of the classical tripos.   In the preceding year his father had married again, a
Miss Susan Barber, whom he cordially welcomed as stepmother; and immediately after
taking his degree he became himself engaged
to his cousin, Fanny Alford of Heale.

" In their summer walks amid the woods and terraces
of Burton," writes Mrs. Alford, "and on the heights
above Sedgmoor, the betrothed cousins framed for
their future life no more ambitious scheme than the
care of some country parish.   They learned to open
their hearts unreservedly to one another; they read,
learned, and reasoned on Scripture together, and prayed
together; they formed, and very nearly accomplished,
in those six weeks, the design of reading together
the first volume of Dobson's edition of Hooker's
Works, his first five books of 'Ecclesiastical Polity,'
and his sermon on 'The Certainty and Perpetuity of
Faith in the Elect.'   Archdeacon Evans's charming
book, 'The Rectory of Valehead,' was twice read
through, first by Henry alone, then by him to his
future wife and her sisters.   The good Archdeacon had
been his tutor at Cambridge, and exercised great influence over his mind at that time.   Henry determined
to enable his future wife to read the New Testament
in Greek, and for this purpose began a Greek Grammar in the form of a series of letters to her, which

grew to the extent of sixty folio pages. For the amusement of his cousins generally he wrote some small pieces entitled 'Guesses at Truth,' &c., and gave them as his contribution to the 'Family Mirror,' a periodical which never attained the dignity of appearing in print, but was circulated in manuscript among various young members of the Alford family. In the enthusiasm of those young days he planned the formation of a society amongst ourselves for the regulation of social intercourse, with the object of avoiding frivolous conversation and giving mutual aid in detecting and correcting faults."

The beauties of Nature, then as always, were his greatest delight :—

> "Beauty and Truth
> Go hand in hand—and 'tis the providence
> Of the great Teacher, that doth clearest show
> The gentler and more lovely to our sight,
> Training our souls by frequent communings
> With her who meets us in our daily path
> With greetings and sweet talk, to pass at length
> Into the presence, by unmarked degrees,
> Of that her sterner sister ; best achieved
> When from a thousand common sights and sounds
> The power of Beauty passes sensibly
> Into the soul, clenching the golden links
> That bind the memories of brightest things." [1]

And especially delightful to him was the scenery of the hill-ridges above Sedgmoor :—

[1] From " The School of the Heart."

> " I would stand
> Upon the jutting hills that overlook
> Our level moor, and watch the daylight fade
> Along the prospect ; now behind the leaves
> The golden twinkles of the western sun
> Deepened to richest crimson ; now from out
> The solemn beech-grove, through the natural aisles
> Of pillared trunks, the glory in the West
> Showed like the brightly burning Shechinah,
> Seen in old times above the Mercy-seat
> Between the folded wings of Cherubim."

Returning to Cambridge in October 1832, Henry Alford took pupils, and in the following spring published his " Poems and Poetical Fragments." In October 1833 he was ordained at Rochester, and entered upon the curacy of Ampton, which his father had vacated to take the rectory of Winkfield. Many misgivings beset him at first as to how he could fulfil his clerical duties. " My inexperience may be in a few years remedied," he wrote to his betrothed wife soon after, " but I feel as if I had no ground to go upon. My fancied fitness for the ministry and my cherished schemes of usefulness have all slipped away, and I am left a mere boy in understanding." And again, after he had been seven weeks at Ampton, " Oh, how the profession of God's ministry and the light of His countenance bring to notice all my many shortcomings, and set before me my secret sins." On November 6, 1834, his journal records :—

"I went up to town and received the Holy Orders of a Priest; may I be a temple of chastity and holiness, fit and clean to receive so great a guest; and, on so great a commission as I have now received, O my beloved Redeemer, my dear Brother and Master, hear my prayer."

In March 1835 the small, obscure, and till then neglected vicarage of Wymeswold, in Leicestershire, fell vacant, with its population of 1200 and an income of £120, and was accepted by him with a view to his immediate marriage with his cousin Fanny, "that dear person, who had been through life the chief object of his love on earth." At Wymeswold he built and superintended the schools, he almost rebuilt the church, and conducted three services every Sunday. He also began to preach the unwritten, though much meditated, sermons for which he afterwards became celebrated. The narrow income of his living necessitated taking pupils, but the extra labour thus involved rendered only more delightful his holiday rambles with his wife, especially their first foreign tour in 1837, described in his Sonnets, which at this time go far to form a record of his life. Of the

quiet happiness of his home life he tells us in
" Every Day's Employ :"—

> " I have found Peace in the bright earth
>   And in the sunny sky :
> By the low voice of summer seas,
>   And where streams murmur by.
>
> I find it in the quiet tone
>   Of voices that I love :
> By the flickering of a twilight fire,
>   And in a leafless grove.
>
> I find it in the silent flow
>   Of solitary thought :
> In calm half-meditated dreams,
>   And reasonings self-taught.
>
> But seldom have I found such peace
>   As in the soul's deep joy
> Of passing onward free from harm
>   Through every day's employ.
>
> If gems we seek, we only tire,
>   And lift our hopes too high ;
> The constant flowers that line our way
>   Alone can satisfy."

During the residence of the Alfords at
Wymeswold their four children were born,
and there, in April 1844, their youngest boy,
Clement, died. " Is not the triumph of having
one dear child landed in glory enough to
comfort the heart even of bereaved parents ? "
the Vicar wrote to his brother-in-law, Walter
Alford.

In 1845 the design of writing a commentary on the Greek Testament had begun to assume a definite form in Henry Alford's mind. He fancied at first that it could be accomplished in a twelvemonth of hard labour; but 1847 found him only advanced sufficiently to have an increasing sense of the importance and magnitude of the work he had undertaken; and after a visit to Bonn in that summer for the sake of German study, he resigned his pupils—having trained as many as sixty, of whom many have since filled conspicuous positions—and gave up to his commentary all the time which was not claimed by his parish. Yet in the fullest sense he fulfilled his parochial duties. Mrs. Alford writes:—

"It was his habit to enter thoroughly into the individual cases of his pastoral work. Some portion of it was necessarily intrusted to his curate, and he took great pains to secure colleagues of congenial spirit with himself. Each soul was treated distinctly as a part of the charge committed to him. Though naturally disposed to be reserved and shy, Henry did not seclude himself from personal intercourse with any of his parishioners if it might be profitable for them. Privately as well as publicly his gentle and winning sympathy was ready to be offered to each one who sought it, whether in joy or sorrow. Nor did he omit to take any suitable opportunity that presented itself to him

either of correcting or of encouraging those whom he
desired to see walking in the way of godliness."

His standard of what he required in a curate
is expressed in the following passage from a
letter in which he asks help in seeking one :—

"I want him to teach and preach Jesus Christ, and
not the Church ; and to be fully prepared to recognise
the pious Dissenter as a brother in Christ and as
much a member of the Church as ourselves. Above
all, he should be a man of peace, who will quietly do
his own work and not breed strife."

In November 1850 the first volume of the
Greek Testament was published. Alford had
thrown his whole soul into it. " His bravery,"
says Dean Merivale, " was manifested in the
unfailing serenity and confidence with which he
encountered his work, and the cheerful, undoubting satisfaction with which he looked both
forward and backward. His mind seemed at
perfect peace, as one well assured that his work
was appointed him, and that he was doing it."

When working at Babbicombe at the second
volume of his Greek Testament during his
summer holiday in 1850, Henry Alford lost
his remaining son, Ambrose. His memory was
always a most precious possession to his parents.
He had lived, to a rare degree, in the purest

light of truth, and he died before the clear stream of his boyish life had mingled with the turbid waters of the world. The boy's danger was only apparent an hour before his death. There were few parting words, but those very sweet ones. His father records them—

> " Refresh me with the bright blue violet,
> And put the pale faint-scented primrose near,
> > For I am breathing yet :
> > > Shed not one silly tear,
> > But when my eyes are set,
> Scatter the fresh flowers thick upon my bier,
> And let my early grave with morning dew be wet.
>
> I have passed swiftly o'er the pleasant earth,
> My life hath been the shadow of a dream ;
> > The joyousness of birth
> > > Did ever with me seem :
> > My spirit had no death,
> But dwelt for ever in a full swift stream,
> Lapt in a golden trance of never-failing mirth.
>
> Touch me once more, my father, ere my hand
> Have not an answer for thee ;—kiss my cheek
> > Ere the blood fix and stand
> > > When flits the hectic streak ;
> > Give me thy last command,
> Before I lie all undisturbed and meek,
> Wrapt in the snowy folds of funeral swathing-band."

In a paper written nearly twenty years afterwards, Henry Alford describes no imaginary scene, but his boy's death-bed on the last day of August.

" You remember when we last entered such a chamber; and on that little press-bed in the corner by the window lay all we cared for; in that room we scarce dared breathe; even grief was lulled, and all was solemnised without a feeling beyond. We stood all four round his dying bed, with the sunset from the western sea filling the room with rosy light; and we watched till the dear features lost meaning and their lines stiffened; and then I pressed down the eyelids, and we left Mama with him, and we three went out bewildered, and sat down on the beach, and I said, ' Where is he now ? ' The sun had gone down, and had left in the lower sky a few lines of dull red, and under them the sea looked a pale ghostly blue, and the sky above was clear, yet without a star. And there was not a sound, not a breath, not a ripple. All seemed to speak of a presence gone. He had been about those rocks, and on that beach, and cleaving those waters—and now ? "

Long after, writing from Devonshire to his daughter Mary, Henry Alford says :—

"*July* 17, 1866.—The journey was long enough. After passing Exeter came the well-known line of red coast and the accustomed **pang** and tears in the eye as a certain bay of sorrow came in sight. Sixteen years ago ! O darling ! what would he have been now ? Yes, but *what is he now ?* "

It was in the old paternal house of Heale, which had witnessed their betrothal and marriage, that the bereaved parents sought a refuge in their grief. Its desolation and decay were congenial to them.

" We are at our childhood's home, a large old house in one of the beautiful sites in the county of Somerset. Everything here is hushed and solemn. .The house is one of the last century, and part of no one knows how many centuries before. The timber is vast and un-trimmed, the boughs waving before and scraping the windows. The front looks up a decayed avenue of chestnuts yearly despoiled of some of their companions, at the end of which is a tall column erected by the great Lord Chatham to the memory of Sir William Pynsent, who bequeathed him the estate of Burton Pynsent, now all gone to ruin, the house fallen down, the garden a wilderness. Add to all this that my wife's father, the head of our family, is paralysed and helpless, waiting his dismissal. In this place we have all grown up and played our childish games, and now it is the centre and resort of the widely scattered members of a family numbering twelve married couples and thirty grandchildren, besides brothers and sisters of the last generation—in all numbering sixty-two persons. Is it not a place strangely in harmony with our present feelings? ' This is not your rest' is written on every mouldering stone of the old house; and to add to all, dear Ambrose was here full of life and spirits only a month ago."

Afterwards, writing to Lady Sitwell, Henry Alford said :—

"I have found that the fact of our dear children having wrestled with and overcome death seems more than ever to remove all terror from the prospect of our own struggle with him. To think that those cherished ones, from whom we have carefully fenced off every rough blast, whom we led by the hand in every thorny path, have gone by themselves through the dark valley; that those weapons of which we had only begun to teach them the use have been successfully wielded by their little hands, and that their victory is gained before it had come to our own turn to prove them. Such thoughts seem to show us the meaning of the wonderful expression, 'More than conquerors.' If they could struggle and overcome, much more we, with so much more knowledge and experience. No doubt our fight will be harder, for the world has wrapped itself more closely round our hearts. But let not our faith fail in Him who has conquered death, and I do not doubt that He who now leads our dear children in the green pastures of eternal joy will in His own time make perfect His strength in our weakness, and show us that all deep afflictions have been in reality our best and greatest blessings."

In 1851–52 Henry Alford was frequently employed as a lecturer, and his lectures, many of which were repeatedly delivered, became very popular. One of them, "The Queen's English," was afterwards published as a little volume. In the autumn of 1852 he watched over the death-bed of his father, his best and earliest friend, the friend whom he always felt to have understood him best. In the following spring came the offer of Quebec Chapel in London, and he determined to leave Wymeswold. To his wife, on receiving the offer, he wrote :—

" I feel deeply that my work at Wymeswold is done ; it has been the work of a pioneer. I have been the means of preparing and working for what is to come ; but, like all others who do this, I am not the man to continue it. Untoward circumstances have thrown me into false positions; and now that my Greek Testament withdraws me from the parish, I have, and must have to the people in general, the aspect of an idle shepherd, letting others do his work ; and after eighteen years, as the generation grows up which knows not Joseph, this must infallibly get worse and worse. . . . First trust me, which I mention only first because it is in this matter the necessary inlet to the other, and next trust God. If we take up this plan, determined to serve Him, not neglecting common prudence, but at the same time, in a humble self-sacrificing spirit, He will bring us safe through, never doubt it; so let me at least have your sympathy. Eve wept over her flowers ; Eve's daughter can do no less. Eve's son will have hard work to get up a dry parting; but sure I am of one thing—heaven's flowers will bloom the sweeter for it."

A letter to his daughter Mary about this time, on their future life, contains the following touching words :—

H

"In the life which is now opening may we be kept
as a Christian family, without any difference or cold-
ness to each other, and each be the means of good to
the rest, as long as we are spared together here! I
feel and know that I am often hasty and wayward
to dear Alice and you, and that my manner and
words discourage and grieve you. This is very sinful
in me; and when you see it, you see that your father
on earth is not like your Father in heaven, on whose
brow there is never a frown, who never is wayward
or hasty. Forgive it, and do not let it discourage you,
dearest children. Pray for me, and I will strive to be
gentle and loving at all times, and to reprove, not with
temper, but with equity and mildness."

And again :—

"Half our little band is already with the Lord; let
us ever so live as those hoping to join them where they
are. They are one with Christ in glory; let us be one
with Him and them in faith and hope and purity, living
by one blessed spirit. Many and sweet are our com-
forts here, deep and blessed our love for each other,
and what will our joy and love be when our circle
is again completed, father and mother, brothers and
sisters, in a glorious eternity!"

In September 1853 the Alfords removed
to a house in Upper Hamilton Terrace, St.
John's Wood, in a situation whose quietness
was favourable to literary work, while the

distance from Quebec Chapel was not too great
for a walk. During the four years of his residence here, Henry Alford's habit was to rise
at six, light his own fire in his study, and
work there till one o'clock. One hour before
breakfast was given to composing his sermons,
and the rest of the morning to the Greek Testament. In the afternoon he visited amongst
the poor inhabitants of his district, though the
principal care of them devolved upon his curate.
Evenings passed at home were spent in reading
aloud to his family, and few read so well or
effectively. His morning sermons were carefully written, and six volumes of these Quebec
Sermons were published; but his afternoon
sermons were extempore. Reading any of the
sermons, however, is not what hearing them
was. He had the manner and the voice which
gave at once a solemnity and an interest to all
he said; his hearers knew that he felt all he was
saying to the uttermost, and his rich stores of
knowledge of theology and literature of every
kind made him especially acceptable to the
cultivated classes who formed the main portion
of his congregation.

Yet, people went to Henry Alford's church
not for an intellectual feast, but to gain help in
living the Christian life. He put forth the truths

on which that life depends. He pictured the life itself, and fearlessly exposed the faults and temptations by which a London existence, especially in fashionable London, is surrounded.

The afternoon sermons were rather a kind of exegetical lecture, embracing the whole context of a passage, and going fully into its connection and argument. Critical questions were often handled, though only as far as the subject in hand fairly demanded. This kind of preaching was then a novelty, though it has since become less uncommon, and the Sunday afternoon congregation at Quebec Chapel was consequently of a peculiarly high order—members of Parliament, eminent lawyers, and other varied representatives of the intellectual classes, to whom the study of a definite portion of the New Testament which was presented to them had an especial interest, as inviting them to verify what was said by the conscientious study of the chapter for themselves. It was known also that Alford was a careful scholar and a diligent student. Men went to him as to one who could render a reason, and who was not likely to rely on a mistranslation in the Authorised Version, either because he had not looked at his Greek Testament before he went into the pulpit, or because he would not have detected the error if he had.[1]

Of these lectures the Rev. E. T. Vaughan writes :—

"The work which Alford did in making these critical and exegetical helps, which had hitherto been the property in England only of a few readers of German, to become the common heritage of all educated Englishmen, was a work which no other man of his own generation could have achieved equally well, or was likely to have attempted. His industry was wonderful, his power of getting through work such as I have never known equalled. No man could sum up more clearly and concisely the conflicting opinions of others; none could, on the whole, exercise a fairer or more reasonable judgment between them. No man could be more honestly anxious to arrive at truth; he shirked no difficulty which he felt; he kept back nothing which he believed. On all critical and exegetical questions he was always open to conviction, and never ashamed to confess a change of opinion."

After having been some months at Quebec Chapel, Henry Alford wrote to his friend Mr. Vaughan :—

"The chapel is full, and the people seem attached and kind, and liberal in contributing to every good work. My morning congregation is, of course, *the*

---

[1] Memoir. Letter of B. Shaw, Esq.

congregation, and for them I write my sermons,
having begun with the year. But the afternoon congregation is the one I love best, being my own child.
It has increased from absolutely nothing to within a
hundred or two of the morning. To them I do not
preach, but expound the Gospels; in fact, expand my
Greek Testament notes, a sort of thing in which, as
you may imagine, I delight much. My district work
is very interesting, and when our schools are once
set on foot, will be much more so. But my situation,
you must know, is no sinecure. I find it difficult to
get time for my Greek Testament work amongst its
duties."

In the spring of 1854 the living of Tydd St.
Mary's, Lincoln, was offered to Henry Alford
by the Lord Chancellor Cranworth. He
comically describes in his journal his visit to
the Lord Chancellor on the occasion of his
declining it :—

"When I asked to see Lord Cranworth, the servant
said his master was engaged. I then said, 'I am not
come to ask for anything, but to refuse something
offered.' 'Oh, sir, then I am sure he will see you,'
was the reply."

When wearied with the work of the London
season, the summer tours of the Alfords in the
Pyrenees, the South of France, and Scotland
were the greatest refreshment. The family

travelled in the simplest and most primitive
fashion, Mrs. Alford and her daughters carrying their necessaries in hand-bags over the
mountains, and the father of the family looking
like a pilgrim of old time, and almost confining
his luggage to a thick walking-stick, which
unscrewed at different points, and disclosed
comb, tooth-brush, &c. &c. In 1856 Henry
Alford became one of the ' Five Clergymen'
of the Clerical Club, who met for the purpose
of revising the Authorised Version of the New
Testament—of which the first publication—the
Gospel of St. John—appeared in the spring of
1857. "In this work he soon won the affectionate esteem of his companions. Thoroughly
versed in the subject, he was not in the least
disposed to dogmatise, or press his own opinion
unduly ; he was quick in catching and appre-
ciating the suggestions and arguments of others,
even when they were at variance with his
own. His opinion on difficult points of criticism,
interpretation, and rendering was always received with respect ; but in general he seemed
to keep himself in the background." [1]

Alford's character in private at this time
" was strongly marked," says Mr. Shaw, " by
three qualities—earnestness, for his religion

[1] Memoir. Letter of Rev. W. G. Humphry.
*

was no mere theory ; manliness, for it never
degenerated into sentimentalism ; energy, for
it abhorred all idleness of mind or body ; his
grasp of the truth he held was very tenacious,
he never felt tempted to go from his anchorage." [1]
One of those who knew him best wrote long
afterwards concerning his life at this time :—

" His bravery was manifested in the unfailing serenity and confidence with which he encountered his
work, and the cheerful, undoubting satisfaction with
which he looked both backward and forward. I never
heard a murmur from him, I never saw him despond,
I never knew him look anxiously about for the means
of bettering and advancing himself. His mind seemed
at perfect peace, as one well assured that his work was
appointed him, and that he was doing it. I knew
many of his troubles, but this brave spirit of his,
anchored in domestic love and religious faith, never
quailed before any of them."

In March 1857, whilst he was engaged with
his family in receiving a drawing-lesson from
Leitch the artist, a letter came from Lord
Palmerston offering him the Deanery of Canterbury, an offer which came just when he was
feeling especially overdone with work, and
which he hailed gladly, as giving him the time
sorely needed for his Biblical studies, as well

[1] See Memoir, p. 497.

as for attending the meetings of the Ecclesiastical Commission, of which he was an official
member, and of the Lower House of Convocation of the Province of Canterbury, of which,
after the Prolocutor, he was the senior member.

IN THE DEANERY GARDEN, CANTERBURY.

Great too was the delight of his art-loving soul
in his new home, in the charming old house
and ancient garden, with its time-honoured
mulberry-trees, nestling under the shadow of
one of the grandest cathedrals in the world.

By the establishment of an afternoon sermon in the cathedral Dean Alford was able to carry out, in some measure, the work for which he had seemed so peculiarly fitted at Quebec Chapel. During his sermons the cathedral was crowded. Few Churchmen, certainly few Churchmen in high places, had ever dared to speak before with his fearless liberality. His position towards the great Nonconforming communities was almost unique. "True to the traditions of his cathedral," said Archbishop Tait, "which offered a sanctuary in time of danger to the persecuted Protestants of the Continent, he was enabled, from his longing after perfect communion with all who served his Lord, to unite with many from whom others are by conscientious convictions separated, and to make it understood that the faithful minister and leader of the Church of England has a heart as wide as the Church of Christ."[1] After one of his sermons a poor woman was heard to say, "And the common people heard him gladly."

In everything the change from London to Canterbury was for the happiest. By the older inhabitants of the Precincts the Dean was at first looked upon as a revolutionist, but the

[1] See the Archbishop's Charge, October 2, 1872.

gentleness of his character disarmed opposition.
Work of the most interesting kind could now
also frequently be varied by tours which were
full of interest, and which afforded him delightful opportunities for the sketching which
was his greatest enjoyment, and in which he
became a facile though never a distinguished
artist. Above all, he was able to finish the
great work of his life, concerning which he
thus touchingly expressed his hopes :—

"I have now only to commend to my gracious God
and Father this feeble attempt to explain the most
mysterious and glorious portion of His revealed Scriptures; and with it this, my labour of now eighteen
years, herewith completed. I do it with humble thankfulness, but with a sense of utter weakness before the
power of His Word, and inability to sound the depths
even of its simplest sentence. May He spare the
hand which has been put forward to touch the Ark!
May He, for Christ's sake, forgive all rashness, all
perverseness, all uncharitableness, which may be
found in this book, and sanctify it to the use of His
Church; its truths, if any, for teaching; its manifold
defects for warning. My prayer is and shall be, that
in the stir and labour of men over His Word, to which
these volumes have been one humble contribution,
others may arise and teach whose labours shall be so
far better than mine, that this book and its writer may
ere long be utterly forgotten."

The close of 1860 finds in the Dean's journal :—

"I am now writing with the ten midnight bells ringing in 1861. God be praised for all the mercies of another happy year, in which I have been enabled to finish my Greek Testament, the work of eighteen years. May He grant that future years, if I am spared to see any, may be spent more to His praise ! If I am to live, keep me with Thee; if I am to die, take me to Thee ! "

In the following spring the Dean paid his first visit to Rome, seeing and enjoying much, and obtaining leave from Cardinal Antonelli to spend several mornings in the study of the Codex Vaticanus, making fac-simile copies of all the principal various readings. Yet he returned to England full of bitterness at the impurity of faith in Rome—in whom "was found the blood of all the saints from Ignatius to the Waldenses,"—and feeling that, with regard to external Rome, after a month one only " begins to see what there is to see." In 1863 he went back to Rome for the winter, taking his wife, a niece, and his youngest daughter with him ; his elder daughter had been married in the preceding year. On this occasion he was even more strongly impressed with the ignorance and superstition of the lower orders in Italy —" their whole creed and practice being pagan."

The completion of the second volume of the
" New Testament for English Readers," and
his editorship of the *Contemporary Review*,
were among the heavier of the Dean's next
few years at Canterbury. The preparation and
publication of his " Family Prayers," his " Year
of Praise," and many articles in *Good Words*
were amongst their lighter occupations. His
hymns, one of which has become the Baptismal
Canticle of the English Church, were always a
great source of enjoyment to him. The chief
events of his home life were the marriage of
his youngest daughter, the birth of two grand-
daughters, and his renting on a long lease a small
country-house, Vine's Gate, half-way up Toy's
Hill from Brasted, commanding a view down
a wooded glen over Lord Amherst's and Lord
Stanhope's parks, and away as far as Sevenoaks.
He took this place partly with the view of provid-
ing himself with a home in case of infirmities
unfitting him for work, in which case he had
decided to resign his Deanery. Always averse
to the dignities of his position, he relaxed them
altogether at Vine's Gate, carrying out especially one of his pet peculiarities, which made him
rebel against wearing stockings at all, or even
shoes, except out of doors, and then of the merest
sandal description.

Those who saw much of the Dean in these years of his Canterbury life retain a most vivid recollection of his conversational charm, as well of his own facility of expression, never at a loss for a word, and the best word, to express his meaning, as of his wonderful power of drawing out the best points in others, and the intensity of his sympathy. Vividly also do they recall the exquisite pathos as well as humour of his readings aloud, and his facility in passing from one subject to another, throwing himself with equal eagerness—his whole being—into the one which was arresting his attention at the time. This was especially the case on serious questions. "As in his writings on great subjects, so in his conversation respecting them, there was a wholeness of heart, a unity of spirit, resembling 'the cloud which moveth altogether if it moveth at all.'"[1] In all his words, as in all his acts, his extreme largeness of heart was manifest. "So you cannot conceive," he wrote to a niece, "how one who denies the Atonement in our sense can receive the Holy Communion with earnestness; but I can. Unitarians, I think, often beat us in their intensely 'thankful remembrance of Christ's death,' regarding it as

[1] Memoir. Reminiscences of Rev. Dr. Stoughton.

Henry Alford.

Dean of Canterbury

the great central act of love, though not in the
sense we do." His own perfect faith at this
time is touchingly shown in his lines on " Life's
Answer:"—

> " I know not if the dark or bright
>   Shall be my lot :
> If that wherein my hopes delight
>   Be best or not.
>
> It may be mine to drag for years
>   Toil's heavy chain :
> Or day and night my meat be tears
>   On bed of pain.
>
> Dear faces may surround my hearth
>   With smiles and glee :
> Or I may dwell alone, and mirth
>   Be strange to me.
>
> My bark is wafted to the strand
>   By breath divine :
> And on the helm there rests a hand
>   Other than mine.
>
> One who has known in storms to sail
>   I have on board.
> Above the raging of the gale
>   I hear my Lord.
>
> He holds me when the billows smite,
>   I shall not fall :
> If sharp, 'tis short ; if long, 'tis light ;
>   He tempers all.
>
> Safe to the land, safe to the land,
>   The end is this :
> And then with Him go hand in hand
>   Far into bliss."

It was typical of his character that, whenever any one took a walk with Dean Alford, he outwalked them. He could not loiter. His rapidity in everything was extraordinary—much too extraordinary. This was especially the case with his rapidity of thought. He often regretted that, write as hard as he might, his pen could not keep pace with his ideas. But his most ardent admirers probably feel that he wrote too much and published too much. Had he been able at an earlier age to concentrate his attention on a few subjects, he might have attained in them to a far higher point of excellence. But he would always throw all his energies for a time into the subject on which he was engaged, and then turn to something else. Thus it is recorded in his Memoir that five of the hymns in his " Year of Praise " were composed on five successive days. He published everything good that he wrote.

The incessant restlessness of action produced by the Dean's activity of thought amounted to incapability of taking rest. It was a real misfortune to him that he had a natural talent for everything—far too many things to admit of his attaining perfection in any of them ; but in his humility about this he was always indescribably lovable. In his little home

arrangements, whether carpentering, upholster-
ing, painting, arranging, decorating, or gar-
dening, he was not so much the planner and

FROM THE DEAN'S GARDEN, CANTERBURY.

contriver as the head-workman. He was enthusiastically fond of music, and looked upon
it as the expression of poetic thought. Often
hasty, he was always generous; and though

I

often ruffled by slight annoyances, he could bear any great trial with more than patient—with happy resignation.

In 1868 Dean Alford published an illustrated volume on the Riviera, to which he had paid repeated visits with ever-fresh enjoyment. Most intensely did he delight in the rich foregrounds of heath and arbutus and pines with which the forest-clad hills near Cannes abound, backed by the jagged line of the Estrelles, the most varied of all minor European mountain chains. At Monaco he "saw hell in all its vice, and listened to some splendid music." On one of these southern tours he had written to his wife :—

"*March* 1866.—I am flitting away from home, a boy of fifty-seven, to enjoy a holiday a boy of twenty-five would despise. It all looks strange and bizarre, but far above it all is an atmosphere of calm sunny thankfulness, causing me to think and feel 'Not more than others I deserve, but God hath given me more.'"

In 1868 the Dean again went to the Riviera, visiting, on his return journey, Ars with its memories of its holy Curé Vianney, and afterwards describing it in articles in the *Contemporary Review*.

Early in 1870 the Dean entered into an arrangement for undertaking a Commentary on the Old Testament, to be completed in five volumes and in seven years, "if life were spared." At the same time he took a prominent part in the Committee for Biblical Revision, which began by Christians of all denominations kneeling and receiving the Communion together around the tomb of Edward VI. in Westminster Abbey. But his health was not now what it was. In the autumn he began frequently to complain of sleeplessness and oppression in the head, and he returned from Vine's Gate to Canterbury in November 1870, with an expression in his journal of "gladness to get once more into the old place, and pleasure after his long hill solitude to see old faces once more." In December his physician pronounced his brain overworked, and that it must have total rest— thus giving a death-blow to his most fondly cherished work.

A few days after he wrote to a niece :—

"After all you were right, and it was a rash act to undertake the Old Testament. The doctor has told me it is too late in life to enter on a new and laborious department of study. . . . As to being low about it, I cannot see it so. If God's good hand has brought me to sixty in vigour, surely all after is pure gain, in whatever form it may please Him to shape it."

And to his eldest daughter :—

"My own view is, a man who has lived to sixty has so much cause for thankfulness, it ought to over-power every other feeling; so it has not occurred to me to be in low spirits. I shall now look up the colour-box and the garden-tools, and the fishing-rods of old days, and take up light literature once more."

But it must have been in the prescience that the blessing of his earthly presence would not long be with them that he had written to comfort his daughter *afterwards* the pathetic lines—"Filiolae Dulcissimae."

"Say, wilt thou think of me when I'm away,
Borne from the threshold and laid in the clay,
Past and forgotten for many a day?

Wilt thou remember me when I am gone,
Farther each year from thy vision withdrawn,
Thou in the sunset and I in the dawn?

Wilt thou remember me when thou shalt see
Daily and nightly encompassing thee
Hundreds of others, but nothing of me?

All that I ask is a gem in thine eye,
Sitting and thinking when no one is by,
'Thus he looked on me—thus rung his reply.'

'Tis not to die, though the path be obscure,
Grand is the conflict, the victory sure :
Past though the peril, there's One can secure.

'Tis not to land in the region unknown,
Thronged by bright spirits, all strange and alone,
Waiting the doom from the Judge on the throne.

But 'tis to feel the cold touch of decay,
Tis to look back on the wake of one's way
Fading and vanishing day after day.

This is the bitterness none can be spared :
This the oblivion the greatest have shared :
This the true death for ambition prepared.

Thousands are round us, toiling as we,
Living and loving, whose lot is to be
Passed and forgotten, like waves on the sea.

Once in a lifetime is uttered a word
That doth not vanish as soon as 'tis heard :
Once in an age is humanity stirred :

Once in a century springs forth a deed
From the dark bands of forgetfulness freed,
Destined to shine, and to help, and to lead.

Yet not e'en thus escape we our lot :
The deed lasts in memory, the doer is not :
The word liveth on, but the voice is forgot.

Who knows the forms of the mighty of old?
Can bust or can portrait the spirit enfold,
Or the light of the eye by description be told?

Nay, even He who our ransom became,
Bearing the Cross, despising the shame,
Earning a name above every name,—

They who had handled Him while He was here,
Kept they in memory his lineaments clear,—
Could they command them at will to appear?

They who had heard Him, and lived on His voice,
Say, could they always recall at their choice
The tone and the cadence which made them rejoice?

Be we content then to pass into shade,
Visage and voice in oblivion laid,
And live in the light that our actions have made.

Yet do thou think of me, child of my soul :—
That when the waves of forgetfulness roll,
Part may survive in the wreck of the whole.

Still let me count on the tear in thine eye,
'Thus he bent o'er me, thus went his reply,'
Sitting and thinking when no one is by."

At the beginning of 1870 the Dean wrote in his journal :—

" Sat up to the New Year. God be praised for all His mercies during the past year of great events. He only knows when my course will end. May its evening be bright and its morning eternal *day*. . . . God only knows whether I shall survive this year. I sometimes think my health is giving way, but His will be done."

The New Year's day of 1871 was a Sunday. He preached extempore in the cathedral as usual in the afternoon. Notes taken down at the time record that he said :—

" The secret of the peacefulness with which the Psalmist went each night to rest, undisturbed by the cares of the past day or fears for the morrow, is answered in the verse—' For the Lord sustained me.' . . . While we heartily thank God for His goodness to us in times past, let us pray to Him still to guide our steps during the year which has just begun, without longing too anxiously for the gratification of our own particular wishes, which must be short-sighted, and may be wrong. . . . It is not for us to consider how many of those present will meet together here next New Year's Day, or what public events may then have taken place. Our duty is only to trust wholly in God's love, casting all our care upon Him, for He careth for us, and to strive earnestly to become less and less unworthy of His love and care."

ST. MARTIN'S, CANTERBURY.

In the following days the Dean suffered much from the severe cold to which he was exposed while attending meetings for the establishment of a Relief and Mendicity Society in Canterbury, but on the 6th he was able to entertain a large dinner-party. On Sunday the 8th he was able to assist in the Holy Communion and to preach, but on the following days he was less well, and on the morning of the 12th, when even his nearest neighbours had only just heard that he was unwell, the passing bell of the cathedral announced that the Deanery was desolate.

Painlessly and peacefully he had passed into the better life. Truly for him, in his last moments, was the petition in his own hymn answered :—

> "Jesus, when I fainting lie,
> And the world is flitting by,
> Hold up my head :
>
> When the cry is, ' Thou must die,'
> And the dread hour draweth nigh,
> Stand by my bed !"

That hymn and another of his own were sung at his funeral. He rests beneath the yew-trees in St. Martin's Churchyard, on the slope of the hill just outside Canterbury. There, where the first English queen built her little chapel, and where Augustine baptized the first Christian king, the dear Dean Alford is buried. His tomb, by his own written desire, bears the inscription—

> " Deversorium viatoris Hierosolymam proficiscentis."

MRS. DUNCAN STEWART

" No spring or summer beauty hath such grace
As I have seen in one autumnal face."

No. 101 is one of the smallest houses in Sloane Street, looking upon the gardens. It was occupied within the last few years by a delicate, beautiful old lady, who retained to the last the graceful figure of her youth, with a sweetness of manner which beguiled, and a wonderful mingling of wit, wisdom, and pathos which subjugated, all who came in contact with her. It was no wonder that many of the smartest footmen in London had often daily to wait for hours round the unpretending door ; it was not strange that the most charming and interesting elements of London society met constantly in the little rooms, or that they were always found and always felt at their best there. Talking of self-respect, Mrs. Duncan Stewart would often quote to her friends the maxim of Madame George Sand—

" Vérité envers le monde,
Humilité envers Dieu,
Dignité envers soi-même,"

137

and would playfully add, " But who should one
be well with if not with oneself, with whom
one has to live so very much?" and the unselfish singleness of purpose which had steered
her unscathed through the vicissitudes of a very
varied life lent a tender charm to her declining
years, whilst her marvellous memory enabled
her to bring forth for the instruction or amusement of her younger friends a ceaseless treasure
out of the rich storehouse of her wealthy past.
Her society was a constant contradiction to the
theory of De Tocqueville, that "the charming
art of conversation—to touch and set in motion
a thousand thoughts, without dwelling tire-
somely on any one—is amongst the lost arts,
and can only be sought for in History Hut."
Sometimes, in rare moments of depression, she
would speak of the pain of old age, of the distress of feeling that she could do so little for
others, of the being "just a creature crawling
between heaven and earth." Yet, with small
means and feeble powers, those who knew her
best remember that there was never a day in
which she did not make some one happy, in
which she had not formed some fresh plan for
the pleasure and welfare of others.

Harriet Everilda was the only daughter of
Major Antony Gore, younger brother of Sir

Ralph Gore, of Manor Gore, in the county of Donegal, who succeeded his uncle Ralph, Earl of Ross, as seventh baronet, the earldom being limited to direct heirs male. Her mother, who was the daughter of a clergyman in Devonshire, died at her birth, and her father soon after. Though of a Protestant family, she was placed for her early education in a convent—Les Dames Anglaises—at Rouen, and there acquired that perfect familiarity with the French language which she always retained. She often thought in French, and entered into the feelings of her French acquaintance as few Englishwomen could do. It was from an association with the surroundings of her childhood that she always said in her old age that it was more natural to her to pray in French than in English.

Upon leaving her convent, Miss Gore went to reside with her guardian, Mr. Gordon, who filled the post of British Consul at Havre de Grâce, and in his house the great charm of her mental powers already made itself felt. Washington Irving and his brother Peter were especially devoted to her. Her passionate interest in everything connected with the stage was first due to their influence. For eleven nights consecutively Washington Irving took her to see Talma act, and in late years she would

often describe the marvellous powers of Madame
Rachel, whom she also saw with him, especially
in the "Cinna" of Corneille—how, as Emilie, she
would sit quietly in her chair when all the
people were raging around her, and then of the
thrilling electric force with which she would
hiss out in the fury of her vengeance against
Augustus—

> " Je recevrois de lui la place de Livie
> Comme un moyen plus sûr d'attenter à sa vie."

It is remembered how, at this time, visitors
at Mr. Gordon's house would ask him where
Harriet Gore was, and he would answer, " Oh,
she is at the end of the terrace making
Washington Irving believe he is God Almighty,
and he is busy believing it."

In her twenty-fourth year Harriet Gore was
married at Paris to Duncan Stewart, a prosperous Baltic merchant, whose mercantile pursuits had taken him to Havre.   He was a
younger son of an ancient Scotch family, whose
clan, the Stewarts of Appin, had occupied and
dominated a large tract of country on the west
coast of Argyleshire from a remote period.
Staunch supporters of the crown since the
twelfth century, the family had been loyal to
the Jacobite cause, and had joined with enthu-

siasm in the wars of Montrose and the risings
of 1715 and 1745. Duncan Stewart's grand-
father was with Prince Charlie at Culloden, his
grandmother and her two children had followed
her husband and the army to the neighbourhood of Inverness in a carriage, and his father
—one of those children—remembered all his
life the carriage being stopped by English
soldiers after the battle, and a little ring being
roughly pulled from his finger. The grand-
father fled to the Continent with the Prince;
the father afterwards settled in Dumfriesshire,
where he bought a small property and became
a deputy-lieutenant for the county. By his
wife, Margaret Graham of Shaw, he had a
large family. The two eldest sons, James and
Charles Stewart, succeeded to divisions of their
father's land, and became active country gentle-
men. Charles, who survived till 1874, was
widely known throughout Scotland as one of
the first authorities on the management of land,
the breeding of stock, and county business;
like his two sisters, he never married, and
lived with them and their aged mother at
Hillside in Dryfesdale for many long years.
Their home was a notable instance of "plain
living and high thinking," and widely and
deeply were they beloved and respected.

The younger brother, Duncan, who, after the fashion of cadets of Scottish families, indeed like Francis Osbaldiston in " Rob Roy," had turned to mercantile pursuits, and in those pursuits had acquired comparative wealth. ever came back with delight to his old home. To that old-fashioned home, immediately after his marriage, he brought his beautiful and brilliant young wife, whose French wardrobe and ready wit were a revelation to the homely Scottish ladies who inhabited it. Though of a thoroughly noble, unselfish character, the venerable mother was almost aghast on first meeting with an element so discordant to the quiet monotone of her long experience, and perhaps went on a wrong as well as a hopeless tack in exaggerating her own homeliness as an example, while the sisters were perplexed by one who, engrossed in the charms of modern literature, unconcern-edly abandoned all housewifely duties to take care of themselves. Time, and the wide sympathies of either side, eventually led to a mutual respect and admiration, but never to the union of intimate affection. Through life, Mrs. Duncan Stewart honoured her sisters-in-law as noble and Christian women, but their tastes and pursuits were always too dissimilar for close intercourse.

Through many years after his marriage, the business in which Mr. Duncan Stewart was engaged compelled him to reside in Liverpool or at a country-house in the neighbourhood. Here the family lived luxuriously and entertained constantly. Economy, at this period of her life, was certainly not studied by Mrs. Stewart; but her husband adored her, and always liked her to do just as she pleased. The Scottish relations grieved in silence, for was she not "just Duncan's wife."

Eight children were born to Mr. and Mrs. Duncan Stewart during their residence in Liverpool. During this time, also, the eldest girl, Minnie, died, after having been nursed by her mother with inexhaustible devotion through a long illness. It was very characteristic of the impassioned character of Mrs. Stewart, that when she saw that the precious life of Minnie had passed away, she prayed aloud—prayed most earnestly—that her child Chrissy might die too, because otherwise Minnie would be so lonely, as she would have no one to play with. She chose Chrissy because she was the child Minnie loved best, and she wished to give up the best to Minnie. When her husband urged her not to tempt God to take Chrissy really away from them, she answered that she had been so rent by Minnie's death that nothing could ever rend her more. Mrs. Stewart, long afterwards, often talked to the writer of her sufferings at this time. She would speak of the difficulty of a living faith, of keeping it alive equally when prayer was *not* answered; she would tell how, when her child was dying, —she knew it must die—the clergyman came and knelt by the table, and prayed that resignation might be given to the mother to bear the parting, and resignation to the child to die, and she would describe how she listened and prayed too, and yet at the end she could not feel it, she did not, and—though she knew it was impossible—she *could* not but break in with "Yet, O Lord, yet *restore* her!"

"Do you know," said Mrs. Stewart, "that till I was thirty I had never seen death, never seen it even in a poor person; then I saw it in my own child, and I may truly say that then death entered into the world for me as fully as it did for Eve, and it never left me afterwards, *never*. If one of my children had an ache afterwards, I thought it was going to die; if I awoke in the night and looked at my husband in his sleep, I thought, 'He will look like that when he is dead.'"

Liverpool was never quite congenial to Mrs.

Stewart. She had many good friends there, but the associates she liked best were Mr. Bald, her husband's partner, and his wife, and a young Mr. Power, afterwards Sir William Tyrone Power, to whose family she was much attached. Men adored her, cultivated her, sat at her feet; but with women, as a rule, she was, in her young days, not so popular. She sought her intimacies mainly in London, to which she never failed to pay a long annual visit, sometimes with her husband, and sometimes when he was away shooting and fishing in Scotland. At that time the centre of a certain literary society of which Mrs. Stewart became an intimate was Lady Morgan, a little old woman of such pungent wit, that Mr. Fonblanque, then the editor of the *Examiner*, used to say of her, "She is just a spark of hell-fire, and is soon going back to her native element." Another person with whom Mr. and Mrs. Stewart were intimate was Madame Jerome Bonaparte, born Paterson, daughter of a father upon whom she looked down, though she delighted to write to him of her *succès de société*. "But he could always avenge himself," said Mrs. Stewart; "he could always write to her— 'My dear Betsy':" it was a terrible revenge. Mr. and Mrs. Macready and Mr. and Mrs.

K

Charles Kean were also amongst the friends of the Duncan Stewarts, and they were well acquainted with the Sobieski Stuarts, whose gallant appearance when young Mrs. Stewart would recall many years after, deploring its change into the " mildew of age." The Stewarts also saw much—perhaps more than many considered desirable—of Lady Blessington, the recollection of whose " perfect beauty" always remained with Mrs. Stewart as a possession. The little circle at Gore House, which was like the court of Lady Blessington, frequently included at this time Prince Louis Napoleon, who was then in exile in England. Another *habitué* was Landseer, whom, with characteristic gallantry, Count d'Orsay introduced with—" Here, Mrs. Stewart, is Landseer, who can do everything better than he can paint." The Stewarts also frequently visited Captain Marryat at his seat of Langham, in Norfolk. Mrs. Stewart always spoke of this society of her youth as " real society," because then people were never in a hurry. One of its most marked features was old Lady Cork, who, after eighty, always dressed in white, with a little white pulled bonnet.

The years spent in Liverpool were enlivened by her intimacy with Mr. and Mrs. Disraeli, who afterwards became her closest friends. Of her first meeting with them she said :—

"One day, when I was sitting alone in my house at Liverpool, and my husband, who loved hunting and fishing, was away after the grouse, as every Scotchman is, a note of introduction was brought in for me from Mrs. Milner Gibson, whom I had known in London, and the cards of Mr. and Mrs. Disraeli. He was a young man then, all curly and smart, and his wife, though much older than himself, was a very handsome, imperial-looking woman. I told them that I should be delighted to show them everything in Liverpool, as Mrs. Milner Gibson had asked me.

"When I went to see them next day at the hotel, I asked Mrs. Disraeli how she had slept, and she said, 'Not at all, for the noise was so great!' Then I said, 'Why not move to my house, for my house is very quiet, and I am alone and there is plenty of room?' And they came, and a most delightful ten days I had. We shut out Liverpool and its people, and we talked, and we became great friends, and when we parted, it was with very affectionate regard on both sides. Afterwards they wrote to me every week, and when I went to London my place was always laid every day at their table, and if I did not appear at their dinner, they always asked me why I had not come to them.

"After Lady Beaconsfield died, we drifted apart, he and I, and though I saw him sometimes, it was never in the old intimate way. The last time we met—it was at Lady Stanhope's—I had a good talk with him though. It was not until we were parting that I said, 'I hope you are quite well?' and I shall never forget the hollow voice in which he answered, '*Nobody* is quite well.' After that I never saw him again, but I had a message from him through William Spottiswoode. 'Tell Mrs. Stewart always to come to talk to me when she can; it always does me good to see her.'"

It was probably on the occasion of the second visit to the Duncan Stewarts at Liverpool, that Disraeli, then comparatively an unknown man, was taken by Mr. Stewart to the Royal Exchange when the place was thronged with merchants at high noon. The scene is a striking one, and it impressed Disraeli much. He said to Mr. Stewart, "My idea of greatness would be that a man should receive the applause of such an assemblage as this—that he should be cheered as he came into this room." At that time Disraeli visited the place unnoticed; but a day came, several years later, when the Disraelis were again on a visit to the Duncan Stewarts at Liverpool, and when he had attained to a prominent position in politics, and he again visited the same place in company with Mr. Stewart. On this occasion his entrance was noticed, and a cheer was raised, which soon spread into a roar, and ended in a perfect ovation. Disraeli was deeply moved. He recalled to Mr. Stewart the remark he had made years before, and admitted, with pride and pleasure, that his ideal test of greatness had been realised.

After many years' residence in Liverpool, a sudden reverse of fortune came upon the Stewarts. The parents went to London, sending their children to the care of an uncle, Mr. David Stewart of Dumfries. This uncle, who soon became as much beloved as he was respected by the young Stewarts, devoted himself entirely to their welfare, though he kept so strictly within their mother's injunction, that, till six o'clock in the evening, he never uttered a word of anything but French, a rule peculiarly abhorrent to his Scotch nature.

After an interval of eighteen months, their father's affairs being again prosperous, the children rejoined their parents in London. They found them established in Wilton Crescent, whence they afterwards moved to a larger house in Seymour Street. Whilst living here, many old friends collected round Mrs. Stewart, and she also at this time became increasingly intimate with Mrs. Delane and Mrs. Milner Gibson. It was probably during this period also that she saw much of Leigh Hunt, of whom she was wont to say that she believed him to be

the only person who, if he saw something yellow
in the distance, and was told it was a buttercup,
would be disappointed if he found it was only a
guinea. Yet these were Leigh Hunt's days of
greatest privation. Mr. Carlyle was very poor
too at this time, yet a friend who knew him very
well, and went often to see him, told Mrs.
Stewart that one day going to Carlyle and
seeing two gold sovereigns lying exposed in a
little vase on the chimney-piece, he asked what
they were for. Carlyle looked—for him—em-
barrassed, and gave no definite answer. " Well,
now, my dear fellow," said the visitor, "neither
you nor I are quite in a position to play ducks
and drakes with sovereigns; what are they
for ? " " Well," said Carlyle, " the fact is that
Leigh Hunt likes better to find them there,
than that I should give them to him."

Whilst the Stewarts were living in Seymour
Street, another of the children, Florence, died.
Mr. Stewart had again suffered losses in business, and the family moved to Smart's Hill, in
Kent, where the mother, with inborn facility,
soon accommodated herself to her change of
fortune. After a time they moved again to a
villa, The Limes, at Croydon.

Meantime a cousin of the Stewarts, Countess
Bremer, who had been lady in waiting to the

Princesses of Hanover, had married, and a lady was temporarily required to fill her place. The eldest daughter, Harty (Pauline Harriet), went for a time, and was shortly afterwards appointed to a fixed post with the Princesses, resigning her place in the home life. It must have been soon after this that her mother wrote to her :—

"My own dear child, I cannot help saying to you that if you ever pine for home, *you must come*—even away from those dear people : it is only for just as long as you are quite contented and happy, that *we* can be *at all* contented and happy to know you—bear you to be away. You are well assured of this, I am sure? My own dear child, our hearts are with you, as yours with us, and all in Christ in God, I hope and trust. But remember, whenever your heart tells you to come home, then we want you, and must have you, please God."

But Harty never came back. In 1865 she married a Hanoverian, the Baron Otto von Klenck, aide-de-camp to King Ernest of Hanover and the Duke of Cumberland, though the bond of intimate affection between her and her mother was never weakened by separation. In 1852, her younger sister, Chrissy (Christina Adelaide Ethel), had been married to Mr. James Alexander Rogerson, of Wamphray, a near neighbour of the beloved uncles and aunts of Hillside.

It was in 1869, whilst he was staying with his brother Charles at Hillside, that Mr. Duncan Stewart became dangerously ill. Mrs. Stewart joined him, and nursed him with the devotion which she always showed in sickness. In November 1869 he died. Mrs. Duncan Stewart was left with an income reduced to the narrowest limits by her husband's heavy financial losses—an income which the devotion of her sons delighted to render sufficient for the maintenance of her little home in Sloane Street. Meantime the affection with which her eldest daughter was regarded at the court of Hanover had led to her receiving constant marks of consideration and favour from the King and Queen, and she was their guest for a considerable time. The blind King delighted in her conversation, and for many years she would save up every interesting story she heard for him. It is remembered that one day she was telling him a story as they were out driving together. Suddenly the horses started, and the carriage seemed about to upset. "Why do you not go on with your story?" said the King. "Because, sir, the carriage is just going to upset." "That is the coachman's affair," said the King; "do you go on with your story."

Of the sad and eventful weeks which saw the
close of the Hanoverian dynasty Mrs. Stewart
had ever much of interest to tell :—

"I was for many weeks with my daughter in the
palace at Herrenhausen after the King left for Langen-
salza, where, like a knight, he desired to be placed in
front of his army, so that all his soldiers might see him,
and where he was not satisfied till he felt the bullets
whizzing round him. The people in Hanover said he
had run away. When the Queen heard that, she and
the Princesses went down to the ' place ' and walked
about there, and, as the people pressed around her,
said, ' The King is gone with his army to fight for his
people, but I am here to stay with you till he comes
back.' But, alas! she did not know!

"We used to go out and walk at night, in those
great gardens of Herrenhausen, in which the Electress
Sophia died. The Queen talked then, God bless her,
of all her sorrows. We often did not come in till
the morning, for the Queen could not sleep. But even
in our great sorrow and misery, Nature would assert
herself, and when we came in, we ate up everything
that there was. Generally I had something in my room,
and the Queen had generally something in hers, though
that was only bread and strawberries, and it was not
enough for us, for we were so very hungry. One
night the Queen made an aide-de-camp take the key
and we went to the Mausoleum in the grounds. I
shall never forget that solemn walk, Harty carrying a
single lanthorn before us, or the stillness when we

reached the Mausoleum, or the white light shining upon it, and the clanging of the door as it opened. And we all went in, and we knelt and prayed by each of the coffins in turn. The Queen and Princesses knelt in front, and my daughter and I knelt behind, and we prayed—oh! so earnestly, out of the deep anguish of our sorrow-stricken hearts. And then we went to the upper floor where the statues are, and there lay the beautiful Queen, the Princess of Mecklenburg-Strelitz, in her still loveliness, and there lay the old King, the Duke of Cumberland, with the moonlight shining on him, wrapped in his military cloak. And when the Queen saw him, she, who had been so calm before, sobbed violently, and hid herself against me, for she knew that I also had suffered, and after that we walked or lingered in the gardens till the daylight broke.

"The Queen was always longing to go away to her own house at Marienburg, and at last she went. She never came back, for as soon as she was gone, the Prussians, who had left her alone while she was there, stepped in and took possession of everything.

"The Queen is a noble, loving woman, but she can also be queenly. When Count von W., the Prussian commandant, arrived, he desired an interview with her Majesty. He behaved very properly, but, as he was going away—it was partly from *gaucherie*, I suppose— he said, 'I shall take care that your Majesty is not interfered with in any way!' Then our Queen rose, and in all queenly simplicity she said, 'I never expected it.' He looked so abashed, but she never flinched; only, when he was gone out of the room, she fainted dead away upon the floor."

Some one who knew her well said most truly of Mrs. Stewart that her life was not a long uninterrupted course, but, as it were, a chain of separate circles. That part of it which belonged to her residence in Sloane Street was what the Scotch call the "uptake," the making of many friendships so infinitely easy to her, one leading to another, until every day was filled by affectionate interests. Yet in the new connections she formed, old friends of former days were never forgotten. Two of those she had long known, on finding her surrounded by a brilliant circle, were once led to say, " Now you have so many friends, you will not care for us ; you must find us so stupid and uninteresting." And long will they remember her cordial answer, " No, no, my dear, you are my *rocks.*" One secret of the great charm of her conversation was that she was not merely careful to evade ever repeating an ill-natured story of any one, but, where there was positively nothing of good to be said, had always some apt line of old poetry or some proverb to bring forward urging mercy—" Mercy, oh, so much grander than justice." The writer vividly remembers how, after once listening with polite self-restraint to a scandalous story about a well-known member of society, she said, with char-

acteristic sweetness, " Yes, he was very fallible,
yet how capable of *becoming* that greatest of
all things, a good man."

In her old age, Mrs. Stewart's strong interest
in the stage was never diminished, and those
connected with it were always amongst her
most cherished visitors, especially Lady Martin,
whom, as Helen Faucit, she regarded as " the
last representative of the studied phase of
acting ; " Mrs. Crowe and her sister Miss Isabel
Bateman ; Mr. Irving ; Mr. and Mrs. Kendal ;
and, amongst amateurs, the not less gifted Mrs.
Greville.

Amongst others whose visits Mrs. Stewart
most valued were Mr. William Spottiswoode,
Mrs. Grote, Lady Eastlake, Lady Gordon,
Mrs. Oliphant, Lady Wynford, Lady Hope,
Mr. and Mrs. Frank Hill, Mr. Henry James
the American novelist, and her old friend, Mr.
Pigott, whom she would describe as being "a
finished critic, but with all the innocence of a
child picking daisies." There was no end to
the variety of different persons and characters
who met in Mrs. Stewart's little rooms, and the
remarkable point was that no one cared in the
least whom they met—they all went for *her*.
Her constant letters to her daughter Harty
show how much she enjoyed this period of her

life, and how much interest she found in it.
Here are some gleanings from letters of 1880–
1883, but they are all undated :—

"Oh, my darling, here are two more days without
any writing. I can only *rest* when people are not here.
On Monday Chrissy had a very pleasant luncheon
party. At a charming party in the evening at the
Felix Moscheles', I fell into a deep admiration of the
Berlin actor, Herr Barney, who is come over to give
added strength to the Saxe-Meiningen company. He
has the finest possible figure and head, crisp, short,
curling hair, and a noble face. He acts Marc Antony
in the ' Julius Caesar ' and seems made for it by nature.
Yesterday I went at four to Madame Modjeska's reception, full, and of interesting people; home for visitors,
dined at Lord Eustace Cecil's, and at eleven o'clock
was at Leonie Blumenthal's, where was a magnificent
party, fine company, &c."

"My own dearest child, I think that it was this day
last week that I despatched my last letter to you, telling
of the good success of my last luncheon. Since then,
life has been too fast for me. I have had scarcely a
minute but for rest during the intervals. At this
season one thing leads on to another, which one cannot
avoid. It is a chain of links ; if one says A, one must
say B, and so on, and so on. On Thursday a pleasant
dinner at Lady Hampson's *led on* to a party this afternoon to see the drill of the Fire Brigade—a most
interesting sight. Captain Shaw invited me and to
bring what friends I chose, and I took three carriages
full. Friday, I was all afternoon at Lady Hooker's at

Kew. Lovely weather. Dear Lord and Lady Ducie took me down, and it was delightful. Lady Martin, who is as good as every one is to unworthy me, takes me to the Meiningen company on Saturday to see 'The Winter's Tale,' so I am well off.

" Dear William Spottiswoode took me down to dinner last night, so it was very pleasant. He told me that Lord Beaconsfield (who meets him every week at a scientific place) had spoken to him of his re-meeting with me, and expressed himself very wishful to see me again. William said I might depend on the pleasure he had had and the wish to see me more. I know *how careful and reticent* William is—so this pleased me."

" *Sunday.*—I am dining out this evening with about thirty persons, all of name and note, at the Boughtons' —not grand fashionable people, but artists, authors, &c. I will write you of it to-morrow."

" *Monday.*—The dinner yesterday was very amusing —guests all more or less distinguished, from Browning down to Edmund Yates and his beautiful wife."

"1880.—Capital company at dinner yesterday. I sat between Lowell and Sir James Stephen, and had a very good time. Among many, Lowell said one bit worthy of the Biglow Papers. Opposite us was Huxley, whom Lowell saw for the first time—'So,' says he to me, 'that's the great Huxley?' 'Yes,' says I. 'Well,' says he, 'in a match between him and God, *I'd bet on God.*'"

" Did I tell you a thing Froude said the other day to me—*à propos* of not understanding, comprehending Tennyson's last poem, the 'De Profundis,' in the last *Nineteenth Century?*—'Wad I presume, blessed sir?'

—the reply of an old Scotswoman to her minister as to a very metaphysical sermon."

"1881.—Tell Mrs. M. how glad I shall be to make her acquaintance. Tell her how very fortunate I have been in having had so many pleasant American friends, beginning fifty-five years ago with Washington Irving, and arriving now at Henry James and Mr. Lowell, both of whom lunch with me this very day to meet the great American botanist, Dr. Gray—indeed, Sir Ughtred Kay-Shuttleworth told me I must say *the* botanist of the world. I have also Lady Airlie, Lady Gordon, &c."

"*Coombe Bank, March 27.*—I am here since Friday with a house full of Arbuthnots and Spottiswoodes, I the only interloper, and they are all as good as gold to me; to-night a large ball, house and grounds lighted with electric light!!"

"After describing his wife's terrible illness, Mr. Lowell said—'My dear Mrs. Stewart, I'd have given Job ten and won.'"

"101 *Sloane Street, 8th April.*—I had a very good time (for, with my infirmities, though much is taken, much remains, I thank God) at Coombe Bank. I drove and walked every day. Kind William Spottiswoode, when he took leave of me—full of thanks and real gratitude, said, 'You bring sunshine into this house!' This was not true, but, as Sterne wrote a long time ago, so kind and good 'that the recording angel dropt a tear,' and obliterated the falsehood."

"I came home last Thursday to a clean house, full of flowers, and dear Chrissy's unceasing care, and troops of friends, *un*like poor Macbeth. I had not been twenty-four hours back till came my dear Caroline

Bromley, Lady Eastlake (so *very* dear and affectionate), Lady Stanhope, Lady Airlie, Lady Strangford, dearest Mrs. Hill, &c. God knows, my child, my lines have been cast in pleasant places."

"*November* 15.—My own darling child, my letters are so stupid they are not worth sending, yet I send them. I see very few people. I have very quiet and delicious evenings reading by my fireside. 'Tis an interval of rest.

"Chrissy is gone down to friends at Brighton. She is very dear and good and helpful and loving and comfortable to me invariably, and I am very grateful and love her dearly, and am very thankful to have her, and lost when she is away."

"1882.—We had a most brilliant day at the Camp. Personally to me it was most charming. I took down Mrs. F. Hill; Lady Brownlow was as good as gold to me, and we saw everybody and everything most comfortably. It was a wonderful English sight. The Duchess of Albany gave away the prizes, and I was close to her and Prince Leopold—saw both for the first time in my life. She is pretty enough for anything, and very sweet and simple. She gave away the prizes charmingly, and smiled more sweetly and simply on the privates than on the generals. This, her first public appearance, charmed everybody. Have you ever seen a Wimbledon camp? 'Tis a beautiful sight! so gorgeous and yet so English!

"I do trust you, my child, for giving proper grateful messages for me from the Queen downwards. God knows how I *feel* them, and so do you, I think. You cannot exceed my feelings.

" My darling, when I look round on my dear children and my dear friends, and *feel* how many hearts and homes are open to me at all times, I truly believe I *cannot* be grateful enough."

The great charm and infinite variety of Mrs. Stewart's conversation were even more felt in country-houses than in London. The writer will always remember one day at Sarsden (Lady Ducie's), being told that an old lady was coming that evening, an old lady who would have travelled straight through from Scotland, and would probably arrive perfectly exhausted. The dinner-hour arrived, and with it there glided in amongst the company a graceful, refined old lady, with features the colour of white alabaster, in a black velvet dress, a chain and cross round her waist, and a lace head-dress which was neither veil nor hood, but so infinitely becoming to the wearer, that from the first moment of seeing her in it, it was impossible to imagine her in anything else. And soon, in conversation, the animation, the inspiration of her eyes, spoke even more powerfully than her lips, and—the next day the whole party were at her feet. Her conversation grew hourly more enchanting. She sat for her portrait in her picturesque lace head-dress to one of her fellow-guests ; she was pleased at

L

being asked to sit—"Il faut vieillir pour être
heureuse," she said. Whilst she was sitting,
she described her visit to Ober-Ammergau.
Her anxiety to go was intense, but, though she
was in Germany with the Queen of Hanover,
all the means seemed to fail. The Princess
Mary of Hanover and the Archduchess Elizabeth *walked*. But, to be in waiting upon them,
went Baron von Klenck, her Hanoverian son-
in-law, and he came back greatly impressed,
and said to his wife when he came in, "If thy
mother still wishes to go, in God's name let
her set forth ;" and she went. She described
the life at the village—the simplicity, the cheap-
ness ; then, in the play, the awful agony of the
twenty minutes of the Crucifixion, the sublimity
of the Ascension. "I have seen hundreds of
'ascensions' on the stage and elsewhere, but
I have never seen anything like that simple
re-presentation."

The following day, at luncheon, Mrs. Stewart
described a sitting with Mrs. Guppy, the spiri-
tualist. Her daughter, Count Bathyany, and
others were present.

"We were asked what sort of a manifestation we
would have : we declared we would be satisfied with
nothing less than a ghost. There was a round hole in
the table, with a lid upon it. Presently the lid began to

quiver; gradually it was thrown on one side, and a hand came up, violently agitating itself. Mrs. Guppy said, 'Dear spirits' (we are always very affectionate, you know), 'would you like the glass?' and a great tall fern-glass was put over the place; otherwise I should have touched that hand. Then, inside the glass (but we could not touch it, you know), came up something wrapped in muslin. Mrs. Guppy said it was a head. Afterwards we were asked to go down to supper: there was quite a handsome collation. A young American, who was with us, was so disgusted with what he had seen that he would touch nothing, would take neither bread nor salt in that house. I was weak. I did not quite like to refuse, and I ate a few strawberries. Of course, as far as the moral protest went I might have eaten a whole plateful. Bathyany took a rose away with him for his Countess, for at the end of our *séance* quantities of flowers appeared, we knew not whence, quite fresh, beautiful flowers: they appeared on the table close to Count Bathyany.

"The spirits are very indulgent. They think we are in better humour if our strength is kept up. After I have been sitting there for some time, they generally say, 'Harriet is exhausted: let her have a glass of wine.' Then sometimes they give us nicknames— beautiful nicknames—my daughter they called 'Mutability,' and me they named 'Distrust.'"

In nothing was Mrs. Stewart more remarkable than in her wonderful memory for poetry, which she would repeat for hours together.

She often spoke with surprise of the general want of appreciation for Byron in England, and would dwell on his wonderful satire, as evinced by his lines in the " Age of Bronze," on Marie Louise and Wellington ; on his philosophy, for which she would cite the lines on Don Quixote ; on his marvellous powers of condensation and combination, for which she would repeat those on the burning of Moscow. But, in all she said, Mrs. Stewart's individuality lent such a power and sweetness to her sayings and doings that any reproduction of them either seems to lose all point, or to be so crude as to give a false picture of her.

Mrs. Stewart afterwards paid repeated visits to Lord and Lady Ducie, and they were amongst the greatest pleasures of her later years. To her daughter she wrote in the great frost :—

" *Tortworth, Jan.* 1880.—I can't tell you all the goodness and kindness I have had, from my Lord and Lady downwards—it passes words."

" 11*th.*—*Tortworth.*—I am so persistently weak and *défaite*, I don't know what to make of it. The doctor says it is not real weakness, but nervous exhaustion. To myself it seems like quite comfortable dying away —no pain, but also no will, no power ; and this is the first time in my life that I have felt myself totally without the former."

"*January* 17.—They shut the gates on me. The cold is so exceptionally severe, severer than for sixty years past, and I am not to be suffered to leave this large house whilst it lasts. It is in vain to rebel, so I put up with my luxuries with patience. I have not been outside the doors since I came, but the house is very large to take exercise in, the company cheerful, and, as you know, I love the dear Ducies. They say they will keep me 'till June and the roses,' if the cold does not abate. . . . I breakfast in my room, go down about 10.30, find everybody brisk and cordial, all the papers, and plenty of the best new books—remain till luncheon at two, come back to my room, rest and books till dinner-time at eight, a cheerful evening—acting, talking, music, and to bed at eleven. I wish you were here, and so does Lady Ducie *heartily*, and then I should have little left to wish for."

A portion of the summer was frequently spent by Mrs. Stewart with her daughter Christina in Scotland, "enjoying entire rest and peace, dallying from day to day, eating lotus (and a good deal besides) with such satisfaction as not to be able to make any plan for moving on." On one of these occasions of long-ago, whilst staying at the place of her son-in-law, Mr. Rogerson, near Inverness, she had made the acquaintance of Brother Ignatius.

"One day while out walking, my daughter met with a young man, of wonderful beauty, dressed as a monk,

with bare feet and sandals. He asked her whether he
was near any inn, and said, 'The fact is I have with
me two sisters [Sister Gertrude and another], and a
brother—Brother Augustine. And the brother is very
ill, probably ill to death, and we cannot go any farther.'
So my daughter made them come to her house, and
showed them infinite kindness, giving them water
for their feet and all Scripture hospitality. Brother
Augustine was very ill, very ill indeed, and they all
remained in or near my daughter's house three weeks,
during which I became very intimate with them, especially with Brother Ignatius and Sister Gertrude. We
used to go out for the day together, and then, in some
desolate strath, Brother Ignatius would sing, sing
hymns like an archangel, and then he would kneel on
the grass and pray.

"Many years afterwards I heard that Brother Ignatius
was going to preach in London—some very bad part
of London—and I went. The room was packed and
crowded, but I was in the first row. He preached—a
beautiful young monk, leaning against a pillar. There
were at least a hundred of his attitudes worth painting,
but there was nothing in his words. At last a little
girl thought he looked faint, and brought him a
smelling-bottle, which she presented to him kneeling.
He smelled at it, and seeing me, an old woman near
him, he sent it on to me, and I smelled at it too. Afterwards I stayed to see him, and we talked together in
a small room, talked till midnight. Then he gave me
his blessing, gave it to me very solemnly, and afterwards I said, 'And God bless you too, my dear young
man.'"

In other summers, Mrs. Stewart was frequently at Hopetoun House, and paid other
Scottish visits with great enjoyment.

"What a climate it is!—just heavenly, no more.
Balmy, fragrant, almost fresh, but not bracing. In
'trim gardens' in the midst of wildness, it seems like
Eden, with wasps instead of snakes."

It was at Lord Ducie's that Mrs. Stewart
first made acquaintance with his cousins, Lord
and Lady Denbigh, which led to other pleasant
visits.

"*Newnham Paddox.*—I wish you were with me in
this heavenly place, with these dear people. You like
magnificence. So do I, when it is not spoiled by
lower things. A. and Crissy do not. We will not
quarrel with them, but I still think that we are right.
This is a really grand place, *le grand air* in everything,
the finest family chapel in the kingdom, I suppose.
Lord Denbigh sold an estate which accrued to him in
Shropshire to build it, and he has done it worthily. I
go in to low mass at 8.30 every morning in my long fur
coat and a black veil—to be sure the chapel is only at
the end of the long corridor. Kindness of every sort
and cordiality is here for me. It is a wonderful sight,
and touching in its way, to see the younger son of the
house, Basil, a lovely boy of eight years, serve the
mass every morning. We are a very small party here
as yet—most cultivated people they are—excellent
music, excellent reading aloud, everybody occupied,

everybody receptive and communicative, every soul
here as yet Roman Catholic, but you know I don't like
them the less for that. I intended to go home on
Monday, but am kept *per force*. I compromise for
Thursday, but I doubt if I get the gates open then, so
cordial, so dear, so hospitable are my hosts—their care
and tenderness to me is nearly filial."

"*Newnham Paddox.*—I wish I could make you
see my visit. Such affectionate kindness, such honour
and respect is shown me, that I cannot comprehend it,
only receive it humbly and with gratitude.

> 'They say this world's a world of woe,
>   And I pity the fools that find it so.'

Here are lines I have found at stately Newnham, and
they strike me as so funny and incongruous that I
copy them."

From 1877 onwards Mrs. Stewart had been
frequently very ill and suffering, and was often
confined for weeks to bed or the sofa in her
little room in Sloane Street, which was constantly brightened by presents of flowers and
fruit, and cheered by the presence of ministering
friends. When she was able, she would talk
for hours on all events of the day with wonderful shrewdness and sagacity, amid which such
gleams of fun would break forth as were in-
describable. Well does the writer remember
some one in her room remarking that an elec-

tion failure which had just befallen Sir William
Harcourt would be as good as a dose of physic
to him, and the sparkling humour with which
she replied, "No ; it would be a dose of castor-
oil administered to a marble statue."

Of her own pains and aches Mrs. Stewart
would seldom speak. "Take care," she would
say, if one had a tendency thus to complain,
"or you will become that most dreadful of all
things, a self-observant valetudinarian. I was
once in a house with a lady who, after talking
of nothing else for an hour, said, 'I won't
speak of my own health, for when I was young,
a dear, old, wise, judicious woman said to me,
"When anybody asks how you are, always say
you are quite well, for nobody cares.'"

From one of her most severe illnesses Mrs.
Stewart declared that she rallied from the time
Mr. Alfred Denison paid her a visit. She had
said to him that she had a presentiment she
should not recover, and he had answered her
that he had never been ill without that presentiment, but that it had never come true.

Speaking of the cases in which the highest
and lowest motives combine, and "Oh, in life
there are so many of these cases," led Mrs.
Stewart one day to speak of the occasions on
which a lie is justifiable.

"There was once a case in which I thought I ought
to tell a lie, but I was not sure. I went to Dr. and
Mrs. Bickersteth, and I asked them. They would
only answer, 'We cannot advise you to tell a lie '—
they would not advise it, but they did not forbid it.
So, when a husband came to question me about his
wife, I equivocated. I said, 'She certainly did not do
what you imagine.' He said to me very sternly and
fiercely—'That is no answer: is my wife innocent?'
And I said, ' She is.' I said it hesitatingly, for I
knew it was false, and he knew it was false; he knew
that I had lied to him; he did not believe me in his
heart, but he was glad to believe me outwardly, and he
was grateful to me, and that husband and wife lived
together till their death. I believe that was one of the
rare cases in which it is right to tell a lie. You will say
that it might lead one to tell many others, but I do not
think it has. Was it not Mr. Stopford Brooke who
once said that 'merciless truth' was the most selfish
thing he knew?"

Another day, Mrs. Stewart spoke again of
how far a lie might be justified by circumstances, such as giving a wrong direction to a
man who was in pursuit of another to kill him,
&c. ; and when some one objected, she dwelt
upon its being far greater to be noble for others
than holy for oneself. Some one observed
that in this case we should all follow the inner
voice, which would tell truly what duty was.
' Yes," said Mrs. Stewart, "having formed

your character by the Master without, you may
then act in crises by the voice within, which
will never be false to your life's teachings.
Perhaps," she added, " I should say, like Dr.
Johnson, I have been speaking in crass ignorance, according to the failings of my fallible
human nature; and yet, may we not all, whilst
acting like fallible human beings as we are,
trust respectfully in God's mercy — though
speaking of no glorious future as reserved for
us, lest He should say, 'What hast thou done
to deserve that?'"

Long in the hearts of those present will
echo the sweet and thrilling tones in which,
after this conversation, Mrs. Stewart repeated
the lovely lines on Mary Magdalen in Moore's
" Rhymes of the Road :"—

> " No wonder, Mary, that thy story
>   Touches all hearts—for there we see
> The soul's corruption and its glory,
>   Its death and life combined in thee.
>
> No wonder, Mary, that thy face,
>   In all its touching light of tears,
> Should meet us in each holy place
>   Where man before his God appears,
> Hopeless—were he not taught to see
> All hope in Him who pardon'd thee.

Often, very often, in these hours of feebleness, would Mrs. Stewart speak and wonder on the mysteries of a future state.

"Do not think I murmur, but life *is* very trying when one knows so little of the beyond. The clergy-man's wife has just been here, and she said, 'But you must believe, you must believe Scripture literally, you must believe all it says to the letter.' But I cannot believe literally; one can only use the faith one has. I have not the faith which moves mountains. I have prayed that the mountains might move, with all the faith that was in me—*all*. But the mountains did not move. No, I cannot pray with the faith which is not granted me.

"I think that I believe all the promises of Scripture; yet, when I think of Death, I hesitate to wish to leave the certainty here for what is—yes, must be—the un-certainty beyond. Yet lately, when I was so ill, when I continued to go down and down into the very depths, I felt I had got so far, so very far, it would be difficult to travel all that way again. 'Oh, let me go through the gates now,' I said, and then the comforting thought came that perhaps after all it might *not* be the will of God that I should travel the *same* way again, and that when He leads me up to the gates for the last time, it may be His will to lead me by some other, by quite a different way."

The kindness of Mrs. Stewart's nature was so great, and she was so appreciative of the good qualities of all who came near her, that no one could help feeling better and a little nearer their ideal when with her, or when they had been long under her influence. To look at the best side of people, and to shut her eyes to their faults, was not with her, as with many, simply a duty ; it was the very essence of her nature.

No one had a more sensitive and grateful appreciation of the smallest present or kindness shown to her by others. Even if the gift was worth nothing and cost nothing to the sender, she would out of the fulness of her heart speak so warmly of the kindness—and with her it was not words, but real feeling—that the giver was often ashamed of how little had been done. It was often almost distressing, however, that she was as open-handed as she was large-hearted. If a person who enjoyed so many pleasures can be said to have had a special one, her special pleasure was to give away. However much a thing pleased her, she would always rather give it away than keep it for herself. Baskets of fruit or flowers, game or new-laid eggs, that were carefully sent by loving friends for her special use, were often looked at and enjoyed for half-an-hour, and then passed on to some friend who would enjoy them equally, and perhaps need them more. It would amuse her children to find that some little object which they had selected for her own use, or some dainty which they had sent to tempt her appetite, had been given away within an hour to a sick friend, or perhaps even to the first person who happened to call. It was not that she failed to appreciate or enjoy the gift, but that with her the impulse to give away was irresistible. Some one said to Mrs. Stewart that one of her nearest belongings would probably end her life in the Queen's Bench from her over-charity and generosity. "Thank God if it is for *that!*" Mrs. Stewart characteristically replied.

Mrs. Stewart retained the happy quality of eagerness about everything to a degree very unusual for her age. To the last she was most eager to promote and participate in any human enjoyment, and her eagerness to help others who needed it was measured only by her ability. She did not ask herself, "Should I do this?" but, "How much *can* I do?" and cold prudence had only a small voice in her counsels. Her kindness, her appreciativeness, her impulsive and sustained generosity, and her eager intelligent interest in everything, created for herself great happiness even in her later personal sufferings; and to one who

MRS. DUNCAN STEWART

asked her, when a book appeared with that title, " Is Life Worth Living?" she replied, "Ay, *to the very dregs.*"

Mrs. Stewart could not endure any language which seemed to her the least exaggerated. Mrs. Kendal one day spoke to her of her being in " the honoured place of age," having reached " the table-land," whilst she and others were only like ants trying to climb up to it. Mrs. Stewart turned sharply round upon her, with— " My dear, you are a fool ; you know perfectly well that no one is old, and that there *is* no table-land."

A visit which Mrs. Stewart greatly enjoyed in her last years was that to those who were then Mr. and Mrs. Alfred Tennyson.

" *Aldworth* (1880 or 1881).—I will write on my first night at this precious house, because I think, I know, it must interest you. Sabine Greville brought me this afternoon by the loveliest of all lovely English drives, really a country fit for a poet to live in. We found here two young Roman Catholics, brother and sister, dear Mrs. Tennyson in all her delicate beauty, and the dear old man. The house is wonderfully beautiful, on a very high hill, commanding the whole country. I am installed luxuriously in three rooms *en suite.* We dined at 6.30. When Tennyson had finished his dinner, he went off. At first I thought he was ill, but everybody seemed to take it as a matter of

course. We sate on and finished our dinners. Then
we moved into another room, where dessert was laid
and the master was sitting with his wine and fruit.
Then, after an hour of very good talk, he went away to
sleep and smoke, she went to rest till 9.30, and we
young ones went into the music-room. Hallam tucked
me up reverently and lovingly on a sofa, and the music
began—real good music, Beethoven and such like. At
9.30 to the drawing-room again, Mrs. Tennyson went
to bed at ten, and he read to us, and it has been a
great enjoyment! Everybody breakfasts in their own
room."

"*August* 31.—Here at Aldworth—a happy day, a
day to note, if I could do it worthily. A deal of good
talk with the master, in and out. A walk by myself
out of the gates. A very good talk with Hallam,
whom I like more and more, and with dear beautiful
Mrs. Tennyson. Hallam sung a German hymn to me,
in his manly true voice, without music, just sitting by
me, in the drawing-room; it was very fine.

"They drove me to a great house, but the drive to
and fro was the thing. Much good talk. I wish I
could remember all, not to record it, for it was very
personal, but to enjoy it. After dinner, the master
was very genial, very confiding, full of interesting talk.
I think I know his character now. He read in the
evening, and now at eleven o'clock I am come to bed,
grateful that I am here, and saying to the time :—

'Stay, for thou art fair !'"

" *Thursday night* (at Milford—Mrs. Greville's again).
—This morning was fine. On going down at eleven

o'clock, I found Mr. Tennyson and Hallam waiting to walk with me; they took me about the grounds, showed me the dogs and horses, and then went off for their own long walk. Dear Mrs. Tennyson was in the drawing-room, and I talked with her till one—very *very* interesting. Luncheon at 1.30, alone with them, and much good and loving talk. I was very thankful, for I felt that they loved me and trusted me. Sabine most kindly drove over to fetch me, nine miles of lovely country, and I felt all love and reverence, and was invited to come back with affectionate urgency. They said, ' This is the thin edge of the wedge; we hope that you will come again whenever you can and will.' All this was and is very pleasant and dear to one's heart, and I *thank God* again and again."

The buoyant nature of Mrs. Stewart enabled her soon to rally even after the severest ill-nesses, but in 1883 her increased feebleness of body, though never of mind, struck all who loved her. Here are a few notes of this time :—

"*8th July* 1883.—This last has been a terrible week—William Spottiswoode's funeral at the Abbey. I had not intended to go, but they sent for me, and I could not and would not shrink. It was a grand and terrible experience. I was so near the grave that I could touch everything and everybody with my hand, and I got so bewildered, that my only resource on leaving the Abbey was to drive smart out into the breezy country to blow off the atmosphere. The day after I went down to Kew (imperative and very good

M

for me), where I could not but clutch fast hold of dear
Joseph Hooker, Lady Eastlake, and even Browning, to
make sure they were still here."

" *Walton Heath, October 9th.*—I came here on
Saturday to my dear Caroline Bromley—a charming
place, full of books and kindness, and care and consideration. We are in the middle of a large airy heath
—a most healthy place, and have the loveliest garden
and orchard that you did ever see, full of sweet-smell-
ing things."

" *November* 4.—I have set up a fine large black cat,
called Joe—a travelled cat. He was in Cairo with the
poor Elliots when they died in one week. Joe is very
fond of me, and will hardly leave my lap. I find him
very heavy, and would often be glad to get rid of him,
but don't like to disturb him : he does not so much
mind disturbing me."

" *November* 25.—I am getting quite fairly better.
Henry James came and sate by my bedside a long
while to-day, and I had a good time. Lady Gordon
was here yesterday, and everybody is very very good
to me. Mrs. Bald sends me beautifully chosen game,
Mrs. Houldsworth grapes and figs—such grapes !—and
the goodness—and the goodness! My maidens, East
and Polly, are as you know them. I hope their mother
is coming up to spend Christmas, and I intend and plan
that they should have a happy time, please God."

In the autumn of 1883, after a visit to her
much-valued friend Mrs. Hamilton, of Brent
Lodge, Mrs. Stewart had insisted, in spite of her
infirmities, upon going to Scotland. Hitherto

she had always travelled third-class, saying it was the one economy she could indulge in without hurting any one else. But this time her loving daughter Christina and Miss Hamilton insisted upon going beforehand to engage a Pullman car and have everything ready. When she arrived, she was as much enchanted as a girl of sixteen, shook hands with the caretaker, and completely captivated him ; washed her hands at once to try the tap ; was enraptured with the furniture, saying her only trouble was whether to lie on the sofa or sit in the arm-chair; and then suddenly she burst into tears, and flung her arms round her daughter Chrissy, saying, "My dear, you should not make me wish so much to live ; surely the angels in Heaven can never take the care of me you do!"

In January 1884, the death of her kind son-in-law, James Rogerson of Wamphray, was a great shock to Mrs. Stewart in her enfeebled state. Soon her weakness increased so much, that her Hanoverian daughter was summoned from Gmunden, and came at once with her husband and children. The mother was able to have pleasure in this last reunion, and the daughter had the unspeakable comfort of having had the power of sharing with her

sister in loving ministrations to the last weeks
of their mother's life here. Before this, Mrs.
Stewart had always seemed to avoid all
thought of death, but now, when she saw and
accepted that death must be the termination
of her illness, she set herself, so to speak, to
examine the process. She evidently had no
fear, and repeatedly spoke of the entire trust
and confidence with which she left herself in
God's hands. She also said in a musing kind
of way, more than once, " It is curious, this
thing which you call dying—this curious thing
called dying." She retained the use of all her
powers of observation till a few hours before
the end, and the whole of the last week was
strongly characteristic of her—her intellect, her
sweetness, her sense of humour, being all seen
as it were under an electric light. A few days
before the end, a dear Roman Catholic friend,
who had always hoped that in her last hours
she might be received into the Roman Church,
came to her, and urged it vehemently—" There
was no time to be lost ; it was not necessary to
understand or receive all the articles of the
[Roman] faith ; all that was really necessary
was to resign one's own will entirely, to say
in humble trust, ' Whatever God wills, I will,'
that would be enough." " Oh, dear friend,"

answered Mrs. Stewart in the sweetest and
most touching manner, "could it be possible
that I, a poor weak woman, could will anything
but what God wills? I love you and I love
much in your religion, and I love God; but
how can I accept technically what I cannot
believe absolutely?" and to this she remained
firm against all entreaties, oft-repeated the last
three days of her life, though, when the same
friend offered to pray with her, she accepted
it gladly with—"Yes, surely we may pray together, to *our common Father.*"

On the 16th of February 1884, Mrs. Stewart
passed peacefully and painlessly into the other
life. Her sons and daughters were with her,
and her two faithful servants. Her last words
were "Higher, Higher," and we may believe
that she has reached that higher existence
where her thirst for life, not repose, meets
its first fruition. Her mortal remains were
laid in a grave of flowers at Kensal Green,
many faithful hearts mourning, many sad eyes
weeping, beside her coffin. East, her maid, to
whom she had ever been caressing in thoughts
and acts and words, only echoed the unspoken
feeling of many as to the common round
of outer events when she said simply, "It is
so terrible that the omnibuses should still

be running and Mrs. Stewart be gone." But a couplet written by a brother of Mrs. Barbauld might be applied to her, who—

> " From the banquet of Life rose a satisfied guest,
> Thank'd the Lord of the feast, and in hope went to rest."

PARAY LE MONIAL

TRAVELLERS often complain of the dulness of the journey through France which they are forced to take in the search after a warm winter climate. They think there is nothing to see between Paris and Marseilles, because they never look. Yet even the traveller who is hurried straight on without stopping might find much to interest him in the rapid transitions—the extraordinary changes in all the characteristics of the country he is passing through. First come the central plains of France; then the rolling hills of Burgundy in the white moonlight; then the great towns, Dijon and Lyons, deep down below and mapped out in the night by their lamps; the dawn over the Rhone valley, with its arid hills and crumbling castles; the change to the blue sky fading into softest amber; the first stunted olives; the white roads leading, dust-surrounded, to the white Provençal cities,

Avignon, Tarascon, and Arles; the desolate
stone-laden Crau, so utterly forlorn that it
seems like the world of another life; the still
blue Mediterranean with its fringes of pink-
blossoming almonds growing in thickets of
asphodel and violets; Marseilles, and its har-
bour and its shipping, and its thousand *bastides*
gleaming snowy-white amid the foliage on the
hillsides; and lastly, the granite phase near the
coast, and its peculiar growth of heath and
lavender, and rosemary and pines. Even the
winter traveller who is ill-tempered and in a
hurry ought not to say that he can find nothing
to admire.

But for those who have time to break their
journey and to linger on the way, no words
can portray the wealth of interest and pleasure and instruction which may be found, and
which too often passes unheeded and unsought,
in the charming little French towns by the
wayside. The writer's own feeling is that his
pleasantest Continental days, those which come
back to him most in dreams, those which he
delights to linger over in memory, are not days
spent in the great well-known sight-seeing
places, Rome, Florence, Venice, Dresden, or
Vienna; not even days amid the greatest
beauties of the Alps or the Pyrenees; but

those passed in lingering in the little wayside
towns of France and Germany.   Seldom compelled to hurry, in annual journeys to and from
the south, short mornings were spent in the
railway, generally in reading up the story of
the places to be visited, and happy afternoons
in rambling about old churches too big and too
grand for the little towns they adorned, in
sketching the ruins of some forgotten abbey by
a willow-fringed river, or hearing some charming story of happy, and often holy and beautiful, peasant life from simple and friendly lips.
Delightful too were the evenings in the primitive clean country inns—not great Anglicised
houses, with the vulgarity and ostentation
which generally follow the word "hotel," and
which always attend the places whither couriers
drag their long-suffering victims, but simple
homes with a welcome from simple hearts, quiet
cheerful wholesome dinners at bright little
tables d'hôte, where the mistress alternately
carved and pressed her home-made dainties,
and where the master formed one of the
company—the humble village magnates, the
doctor, the attorney, perhaps the mayor, and
sometimes a stranger or two, making up the
rest of the party.   And then would come the
rest in snowy beds, whose sheets were scented

with lavender, in little rooms with brick floors
and a single strip of carpet, and a china *bénitier*,
with a bunch of box blessed on Palm Sunday,
hanging against the whitewashed wall at the
bed's head; and the being awakened by the
hostess calling her chickens under the window,
to the rippling of the river through the orchards,
and the sweet scent of the lime-flowers which
hung over the little garden.

Such days as these may be spent at many
of the places between Paris and Marseilles—at
Fontainebleau, with its delightful palace-garden
and its green forest alleys; at Sens, with its
grey cathedral and memories of Becket; at
Auxerre, with its excursions to the abbeys of
Pontigny and Vezelay; at Tonnerre, with its
interesting churches and hospital and tombs;
at Montbard, with its lovely river and its
beautiful abbey of Fontenay; at Dijon, with
its delightful walk to the hill of Fontaines; at
Nuits, with its glorious old church and its ex-
cursion to Citeaux; at Beaune, with its chest-
nut-girded ramparts and mediæval streets; at
Autun, with its Roman remains and glorious
cathedral; at Villefranche, for the sake of Ars
and its memories, and at many places farther
on, and, being more in the south, perhaps better
known than these.

Circumstances certainly have a strange power of gilding, and there are companionships which make almost all scenes beautiful, and which seem to gather up the flowers of life and weave them involuntarily into a garland of perfect happiness. When the golden cord which twined it is broken, the garland withers. Nothing can ever be quite the same again, the delicate lines seem washed out of the picture, the pathos lost which made the poem, and yet, even then, it will often be found that Nature, especially in her quiet moods (and under the expression Nature, one may be allowed to mean all old "unrestored" buildings, for which Time has done more than even the builder), has a wonderful power of comfort and companionship.

Once I was alone at Macon, where we had often been before.

Macon is one of the places which people find most fault with, but which we have always liked. It has so completely a character of its own, with its long quay of quaint houses, two miles long I should think, facing the immense river, which has nothing beyond it, but which makes a great angle just fronting the centre of the town, and so sweeps all its impurities away to the rich distant pasture-lands, and leaves you to that fresh pure air which is now looked upon as a

cure for Roman fever, and which is perfectly
impregnated in May and June with the scent of
lime avenues; for here as well as at Tonnerre
people cultivate the lime-flowers—*tilleuls*—and
gather them in a regular harvest, to dry and
sell to the apothecaries to mix with their *tisanes*.
Indeed no old French wife who knows her duty
ever dreams of being without a good supply of
dried *fleurs de tilleul* to take in boiling water,
with a *feuille d'oranger* and a teaspoonful of
Eau de Melisse des Carmes, for a cold, or
hysteria, or indigestion, or sleeplessness, or
headache, or . . . almost everything.

The ruined cathedral of Macon, battered to
pieces at the Revolution, stands with its two
octagonal towers looking down upon the quiet
market-place. The back part of the town is so
deserted, so silent and grass-grown, that you
might think you were in a Spanish city. The
high walls of convents, with richly wrought
heavy rails before the windows, throw a gloom
over the narrow streets. Here and there the
lines of houses are broken by a courtyard with
acacias and lilacs, before one of the ancient
Hôtels, which in winter receive the provincial
noblesse. The whole life of Macon seems to
be concentrated by the river-side, which is the
scene of constant change from the quantity of

merchandise from the south of France, and the produce of the Maconnais vineyards, which is always being disembarked or embarked. Here also, for those who know the beauty of simple lines, there is a charm in the country seen beyond the river :—

> " Large and strange,
> Crossed everywhere by long thin poplar-lines,
> Like fingers of some ghastly skeleton-hand,"

pointing at the town. There is a charm, and a great one, in the Inn, which faces the broad gleaming water, to which you look across the rugged pavement of the street, between great green boxes, set out on the edge of the pavement, and planted with huge tufts of white marguerites and Portugal-laurels clipped round to look like orange-trees.

In the end of May there is always a great fair at Macon, which is resorted to by the whole country-side. Then the usually quiet town assumes a festal aspect, the walks under the lime-trees are lined with booths filled with gay wares and most brilliantly lighted towards evening, and in the little *place* are numbers of shows—theatres, and operas, and horsemanship—at one *sous* of entrance money, between which a merry crowd wanders and laughs and chatters, entering first *Le Théâtre de Jésus*, and then rushing to see *La Vraie Femme à la Barbe*, who is exhibiting next door. The most popular, and certainly the most exciting, of all these spectacles on our last visit was the Massacre of the Innocents, but then three *sous* were charged for that. It was an awful *tableau*. Soldiers were holding numbers of little children, without a vestige of garments, head downwards by their feet; some were being slaughtered and apparently pouring with blood, while others were lying weltering in their gore at the feet of their agonised mothers. It was wonderfully done—far too horrible, and much more vivid than the famous picture of Guido. The crowd at the fair was so great and the weather so beautiful, that late at night, when the little theatres were all closing, and the shops were putting away their wares, Macon invented a new amusement, a fiery regatta on the broad limpid river,—boats which chased each other, wreathed from end to end with garlands of coloured lamps, reflected a thousand-fold in every little riplet. They pursued, they escaped, they turned, they pursued again, the crews sang and the people cheered, and, as our landlady said, "*il avait l'air tout-à-fait Venitien.*"

But lately the peasants who have come into the Macon fair from the neighbouring towns— from Bourg, and Chagny, Chalons, Autun, and Lyons—have extended their journey a little farther, and taken the opportunity of mingling a religious duty with a secular one, by making the pilgrimage to the shrine of Paray le Monial, which has only lately become a familiar name to Protestant England, though in France it has long been honoured.

Since 1864, when the nun Marguerite-Marie Alacoque, who had died in 1690, received the tardy honours of "beatification," the interest in the place where her life was spent and where she lies buried has been gradually and steadily increasing. Before this, its noble old church attracted few but local visitors, and in England it was quite unknown : in Murray's Handbook it was not even mentioned. But the erection and opening of a new church above the grave of the saintly woman in June 1866, and the announcement in the following September that steps were being taken at Rome for her future canonisation, became the signal for an extraordinary *furore* about her. English Catholics began to say to one another, " We must increase the devotion to the Mère Marguerite-Marie Alacoque ; this

is a thing to be done,"—and no energy has
been wanting to fan the flicker of enthusiasm
about her into a flame, which finally blazed
forth at the time of the Sardinian occupation
of Rome, when the neglected and almost lost
saint was invoked by a myriad voices, and her
intercession sought in favour of the dethroned
Pope, who was even then employed in doing
her honour. Since then the "devotion" has
grown in a way which is simply marvellous.
By dint of preachings and persuasions, pilgrimages in her honour were established in
1873 even in unenthusiastic England (though
it must be owned that many of the *nominal*
"pilgrims" paid their visits by proxy), and in
France processions with banners and chaunts
streamed forth from every province in honour
of the poor nun who had died nearly 200 years
before, and with the hope of her influence in re-
establishing the temporal kingdom of the Pope.

For a long time Paray le Monial was only
accessible by a branch line from Chagny, but
now it has its own separate line from Macon,
which is only used by the pilgrims and by the
working people of the country.

The district this railway passes through
must be bleak and bare in winter, but in
summer it is charming. The undulating up-

lands swell into free heights covered with heath or golden with broom, while here and there a granite fragment crops up above the short grass. The lower slopes are rich with vineyards, the vines being tied to low posts and cut close to the ground. At wide intervals come the villages clustering round their churches, which are almost always more or less picturesque. In the hollows, poplars fringe the abundant streams, and rows of luxuriant walnuts mark the divisions between the fields of clover and lucerne. By the side of the railroad the common flowers of France grow together most luxuriantly — scabious, salvia, mignonette, hawkweed, and here and there masses of dark blue columbine.

It is the country where the childhood of Lamartine was spent, and of which he gives so vivid a description in his "Confidences." One may still see amid its trees the low pyramidal spire at his paternal home of Milly. One may follow the stony path which he describes as winding from door to door between the cottages amid which the little château stands like a great pillar of blackened stone, in its tiny garden surrounded by a low dark wall, behind which the hill begins to rise at once imperceptibly—treeless, shrubless, yet green

N

in summer with vines. "This was all," wrote Lamartine—"yet it is that which sufficed for so many years for the happiness, the thoughts, the peaceful work and leisure of my father, my mother, and their eight children. It is that which now forms the centre of their recollections. It is the Eden of our childhood, and we could wish that the world began and ended for us with the walls of this poor enclosure."

Not far distant we may also see Monceaux, the château which was the home of Lamartine's later life. It stands beautifully situated on a rising ground amid the vineyards, surrounded by tall trees. In 1870 the writer was present there at the sale, when all the sacred household relics were first exposed to the curiosity of the country-side and then put up to auction in the little chestnut avenue, where the bidders sat pleasantly all through the hot summer day upon the grass; and he secured as a precious memorial, for a few francs, the old green satin quilt which covered the bed of the sweet woman whose saintly life is laid open to us in *Le Manuscrit de ma Mère*. After reading her journal, the whole of this country seems fragrant with the recollection of her, and it was over these hills that the peasantry of Milly carried their beloved mistress at midnight, through the deep untrodden snow, to her last resting-place at Saint-Point.

There are numbers of old châteaux like that of Monceaux dominating the Maconnais vineyards, simple old country-houses, distinguished by their manorial dovecotes, and standing on heights in an enclosure surrounded by a wall. The owners are quiet folk, often proud enough of their "blue blood;" but leading simple, sleepy lives, with few other diversions than occasional visits to neighbouring châteaux, as sleepy as their own, and only a few miles distant, or the being occasionally joined by the priest or the doctor in a game of bowls upon their terrace.

As we advance into the hills, the lines of poplars draw together as the uplands close in. Here is Cluny with its glorious Benedictine abbey, of which so large a portion remains— the abbey which furnished the line of German pontiffs to the Papacy, and trained its Prior Hildebrand for the Papal throne and placed him upon it.

The train stops everywhere. It has superseded all other means of locomotion in this quiet agricultural country, and it is the country people who are considered. At all the stations are groups of working men getting in and out

in their blue blouses, and women in their blue
aprons and their caps with flapping crimped
white fringes. Endless are the little excursions which the train makes out of each of
the stations, returning to it again before it
finally moves on. But in the train, besides
the country people with their baskets and
umbrellas (of course we are going second
class—and how much the pleasantest class it
is!) are Sisters of Charity, priests with their
breviaries and ever-moving but silent lips, and
women in the Macon head-dress—the lofty
little tower of straw, rising from a brim shaded
by long black lace lappets; and all these are
on pilgrimage.

The country opens again now. The fields
are pasture-land, mistletoe grows in the orchards, the vegetation becomes poorer, and
here, stranded on the wind-stricken upland, is
a brown Burgundy town, with high roofs and
dormer windows. It is Paray le Monial.

At the close of the seventeenth century,
when the rapid growth of Jansenism was
agitating the Roman Church, the Jesuit party
sought for some new influence which might
stimulate the flagging energies of ultra-Roman
Catholicism. This influence was unexpectedly
found in a poor nun of Paray le Monial, who

came, like St. Catherine of Siena, though by a
very different path, and partly under the influence of the strangest fanaticism, to the rescue
of her Church, as the foundress of the new
form of devotion known as the "Adoration of
the Sacred Heart."

PARAY LE MONIAL

The Order of the Sisters of the Visitation, a
branch of the Carmelites, had been founded by
St. François de Sales, and one of their convents was early established at Paray. Here
was received as a nun, in her twenty-third year,

in 1671, Marguerite, the daughter of Claude Alacoque, a small proprietor at Veroure, near Autun, and of Philiberte Lamyn, his wife. On entering the convent, Marguerite adopted in religion the name of Marie, which she affixed to her own. From the age of four she is said to have been devoted to pious thoughts and acts, and she had always loved solitude. Her parents had wished her to marry, and on finding her impracticable, besought her, in choosing a convent, to join the Ursulines of Macon, whose abbess was her relation; but she insisted upon selecting an Order more exclusively devoted to the honour of the Virgin.

Being of delicate health, and suffering cruelly from self-inflicted macerations, Marguerite-Marie Alacoque soon fell into a visionary state, which increased till her religious transports began to take a miraculous form. Even then there is something most sincere and touching in her desire to shrink from notoriety, and her own simple dread lest her fancies should be delusions. "I constantly fear lest, being mistaken myself, I should mislead others," she wrote to her confessor. "I pray constantly to God that He will permit me to be unknown, lost, and buried in lasting oblivion. My Divine Master has required of me by my obedience that I should write to you, but I cannot and do not believe that it can be His will that any recollection should remain after death of so pitiful a creature."

She appears to have forgotten all else in the longing after a complete heart-union with her Saviour. " I desire," she wrote to one who asked her advice, "nothing more than to be blind and ignorant as regards human affairs, in order perfectly to learn the lesson I so much need, that a good nun must leave all to find God, be ignorant of all else to know Him, forget all else to possess Him, do and suffer all in order to learn to love Him."   Many of her letters now exist, of which a great portion were written to a certain Father La Colombière, who was then living in St. James's Palace, as one of the chaplains of Catherine of Braganza, Queen of Charles II. Those who read them will feel that, however imaginative and ecstatic she was, she had at least a firm faith in the facts and feelings she narrates, and a simple anxiety that while she, the instrument, was forgotten, the narration of them might redound to the glory of God.   In the early part of her life at the convent, she seems to have been really anxious to counteract by honest practical work the increase of her visionary tendency, and we find her in turn fulfilling the offices of "infirmarian," "mistress of the children," and "mistress of the novices." Many of her letters at this time might be mistaken for those of St. Teresa ; for instance :— "I would wish to love my Love with a love as piercing as that of the seraphim, and I should not grieve if it must be from Hell that I should love Him thus." And again :—" Nothing that the world can give would be more pleasing to me than the cross of my Divine Master, a cross exactly like His, that is, heavy, ignominious, painful, comfortless, pitiless. Others have the happiness of mounting with the Divine Master upon Tabor, but I am content to know no other path than that of Calvary, to spend my whole existence amid the thorns, the nails, the blows of the cross, with no other pleasure than that of knowing that this world has no pleasure to give me." Yet shortly after her writing thus, the simple truth of her natural character is shown by her adding—"Alas! how I fear that this very thirst for suffering may perhaps in itself be a temptation of the Devil."

"As to her prayers for suffering," rather quaintly says one of her biographers, "they were most abundantly answered. Her life in the convent was one of constant and acute pain ; agonising neuralgia and rheumatism allowed her no rest, and her only comfort was in frequent communion—what she called the reception of 'the Bread of Love.'"

"I have such a thirst for communion," she wrote, "that I feel if I had to reach it barefoot through a path of flame, it would cost me nothing in comparison of being deprived of it."

Gradually, as her sickness and her self-inflicted penances increased, her religious fervour began to border upon insanity. That which might profitably be understood in an allegorical sense was by her taken as an actual and literal occurrence. Her Saviour, she believed, constantly spoke to her. He addressed her from the Sacrament of the Altar ; He met her beneath the walnut-trees in the garden ; He showed her His wounds, which He said were still bleeding from the persecutions of living unbelievers. He told her that the hour of divine vengeance was at hand, and she interceded with Him, as Abraham did with the Almighty on behalf of Sodom and Gomorrah. One day He said to her, "I search a victim for my heart, who will offer herself up as a sacrifice for the accomplishment of my designs." Then in her "longing after the presence of divine love," she offered her own heart to the Saviour,

and He accepted it.   Visibly and actually, as
she believed and described (always under
the promise of secrecy to those who swore it
and immediately betrayed it), visibly and actually the Saviour received her heart, and
placed it within His own, which she said that
she "saw through the wound in His sacred
side, and that it was burning like the sun, or
like a fiery furnace."   Her own heart at the
same time appeared "like an atom which was
being consumed in this furnace."   And when
it was entirely aflame "Our Saviour placed it
again in the side of His servant," saying,
"Receive, my beloved, the pledge of my love."
From this time Marguerite-Marie was possessed
by one idea alone—the promulgation of the
worship of the Sacred Heart of Jesus in its
actual and literal sense.   Persecuted at first,
and laughed at by her own Sisterhood, she
gradually gained an ascendancy over them, and
henceforth believing that God had given her
a mission to accomplish, she threw aside, in
what she fancied to be His cause, all feelings
of personal reticence, urging upon the world, in
her letters and words, the adoration of the
Sacred Heart, and announcing the eleven
benefits which her vivid imagination assured
her that her Saviour had verbally promised to

those who would honour Him under this
peculiar form :—1. All the graces necessary
for their condition of life.   2. Peace in their
families.   3. Consolation in their sufferings.
4. A refuge in Christ during their life, and
more especially at their death.   5. Abundant
blessings on all their enterprises.   6. That
sinners should find in the Sacred Heart the
source and infinite ocean of piety.   7. That
through it tepid souls should become fervent.
8. That by it fervent souls should be raised
to a higher perfection.   9. That Christ would
bless all houses in which the image of His
Sacred Heart was set forth and honoured.
10. That he would give to priests devoted to
the Sacred Heart the power of melting the
most hardened hearts.   11. That those who
spread abroad this devotion should have their
name indelibly written upon the heart of their
Saviour !

Fortunately perhaps for the world and for
herself, from the time of her "revelation" the
health of Marguerite Alacoque failed rapidly.
She was never free from a burning pain in her
side, which on Fridays was increased to agony.
When she knew that she was dying, with the
ecstatic fervour of stronger days she implored
the nuns not to attempt to alleviate her anguish,

saying that "the last moments of suffering were only too precious to her, and that she had still the longing which had always possessed her of living and dying upon the cross." She died October 17, 1690, in her forty-third year, and the eighteenth of her religious profession. Her last words were—" I have now nothing left to do, but to lose my breath in the Sacred Heart of Jesus."

The first important disciple of Marguerite Alacoque was her correspondent La Colombière, who believed that her message was of heavenly origin, and solemnly consecrated himself to the devotion of the Sacred Heart. In 1678 she had the happiness of hearing that, in the Monastery of the Visitation at Moulins, the worship of the Sacred Heart had commenced, though at Paray it was not inaugurated till six years after her death. In 1697 Queen Mary Beatrice, then exiled in France, was persuaded by the Jesuits to implore the Papal authority to institute a festival in honour of the " Sacred Heart of Jesus ;" but her petition was rejected, and authority for the " Adoration of the Sacred Heart " was only obtained in 1711 from Clement XI. Yet meanwhile, by the indefatigable exertions of the Jesuits, the " devotion " had already become most popular, and the extraordinary

dimensions it has assumed since then are such
that there is now scarcely a cottage or a room
in a humble inn in France or Italy which is
not decorated with a common gaudy print of
the "Sacred Heart of Jesus." On August 23,
1856, an apostolic decree of Pius IX. made
the fête of the "Sacred Heart" obligatory upon
the whole Catholic Church. For a time it
seemed as if the wish of Marguerite Alacoque
was to be fulfilled, and that she herself was to
remain forgotten, while the doctrine for which
she had laid down her life was received everywhere. But her convent companions, seeing
how great, though subtle, her influence had
been, watched over the grave where she was
laid, and in 1703 her tomb was opened and
her body enclosed in an oak coffin. When the
sisterhood were expelled from their convent
at the Revolution of 1792, they took her bones
with them, and for some time they were concealed in the paternal home of one of the
sisters at La Charité sur Loire. It is interesting, however, that, even during the dispersion,
the nuns regularly assembled in the deserted
chapel at Paray on the day and hour of her
death, to sing hymns in her honour. After
their return, bringing back the body of Marguerite, the Bishop of Autun was induced to

allow an inquiry to be instituted into the life
and miracles of " the servant of God." Three
alleged miracles out of many were selected for
strict investigation, all being instantaneous
cures of nuns from shocking internal disorders
upon touching her bones! The examination
proved satisfactory, and in 1824, Leo XII.
saluted Marguerite-Marie by the title of Venerable ; in 1863 Pius IX. gave her the additional
honour of Beatification ; her canonisation is
still to come.

Paray in its present state is one great shrine
to Marguerite-Marie Alacoque. It *exists* by
the pilgrimages in her honour. Half its houses
are inns or lodgings for the pilgrims. Two-
thirds of its shops are for the sale of medals,
prints, or biographies of *La Bienheureuse.* Its
grand old romanesque church—*La Paroisse*
—stands by the river side with two tall towers
on either side of the gable of its west front,
and, at the east end, a great apse diverging
into a whole succession of little apses. Inside,
it is a noble cruciform round-arched church,
pure and beautiful. The only peculiar feature
is the magnificent ancient font, now used as a
bénitier, and surmounted by a crucifix. All
around in groups, and behind the high altar
in masses, are the banners offered to the

"Sacred Heart of Jesus," chiefly of white satin, fringed and embroidered with gold. Some of these are from towns, some from congregations in Paris, but by far the greater number from small country parishes—painfully and laboriously contributed by peasants, chiefly

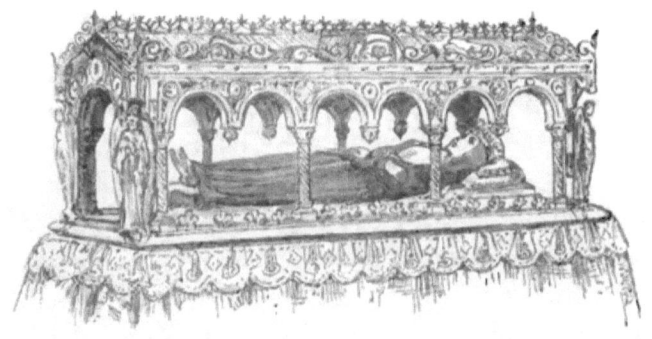

SHRINE OF MARGUERITE-MARIE ALACOQUE.

Bretons. The clean but rugged street winds up the hill to a picturesque old town-hall and the quaint tower of St. Nicholas; but it is only a few steps from *La Paroisse*, between shops full of rosaries and relics, to the iron grille which screens the Church of the Visitation. This is the *sanctum sanctorum*. It is covered with colour and gilding. Day as well as night numberless candles blaze ceaselessly around the shrine.   Against the walls hang ranges of banners even more splendid than those we have already seen.   That of Alsace, adorned with a cross, and the motto " In hoc signo vinces," is hung with crape.   Over the altar is a modern picture of the event which is supposed to have taken place so often on that very spot, the appearance of Our Saviour to Marguerite-Marie.   Beneath lies her body in a golden shrine beautifully decorated with enamel.   It is dressed in the habit she wore in life, and is formed from the still-perfect bones, enclosed in a waxen image.   One portion of the actual flesh is believed to remain intact ; it is that portion of the head which is supposed to have rested, like that of St. John, on the bosom of the Saviour.   The shrine of Marguerite, as it is now, almost forms the altar, and thus, as one of her poor devotees said, " The grave of the Bienheureuse serves as a pedestal for the Throne of the Sacred Heart."

The convent adjoining the chapel is little changed from the days when Marguerite-Marie inhabited it.   The corridors have been painted by the nuns with scenes from her life.   The Chapter-House remains where she was so often questioned about her visions, and the Infirmary where she died. In the garden we may still see the group of walnut-trees where she is affirmed to have laid her head upon the bosom of her Saviour, and the little "Chapel of the Apparition," erected on the spot where her heart is supposed to have been inflamed by actual contact with the Sacred Heart of her devotion.

As we sate in the chapel, one group of pilgrims after another came in, and approached the shrine upon their knees and kissed with reverence the relics, and murmuring voices repeated one of the authorised collects of the Beatified :—" O Lord Jesus Christ, who hast revealed in a wonderful manner to the Blessed Virgin Marguerite the impenetrable riches of Thine heart ; grant, that by her merits and her example, loving Thee in all and above all, we may become worthy to dwell eternally in the same Sacred Heart."

Printed by BALLANTYNE, HANSON & Co.
Edinburgh and London

O

www.ingramcontent.com/pod-product-compliance
Lightning Source LLC
Chambersburg PA
CBHW030107030726
47498CB00007B/2283